SENIOR LIVING – SENIOR MURDER

A Betty Nelson Mystery

BY

Fay La Vigne

All rights reserved. No part of this book may be reproduced or transmitted in any form or by any means, electronic or mechanical, including photocopying, recording, or by any information storage and retrieval system, without permission from the copyright owner.

This is a work of fiction. Names, characters, places and incidents either are the product of the author's imagination or are used fictitiously, and any resemblance to any actual persons, living or dead, events, or locales is entirely coincidental.

This book was printed in the United States of America.
Copyright © 2017 Fay La Vigne

ISBN-13:978-1979004497
ISBN-10:1979004498

Acknowledgements

I would like to thank my family for standing by me during this arduous process of writing my first mystery novel. My sister and her husband, Jane and Bruce Warren, listened to me read chapter after chapter and encouraged me to continue writing, laughed in the appropriate places, and offered important advice.

I could have never accomplished this feat it weren't for my Monday night writing group: Marilyn, Anne, Ruth, Andrea, Patty, and of course, our fearless leader, Char Torkelson. Without her support and encouragement, I would have given up months ago. When I wanted to stop because I hit a writing block, Char always encouraged me to keep going and offered advice about how to work my way back to my computer. She edited my manuscript, help me design and choose a cover, and led me through the publishing process. None of this would have happened without Char. Thank you so much.

To my friends who allowed me to put them on hold when I was busy writing, I promise to show you much more attention now that this book is finished. Thank you for your patience and love.

Lastly, I want to thank my 6th grade teacher at Groveland Elementary School in Minnetonka, MN. Miss Ferber was one of the first people in my life to appreciate my writing and encouraged me to continue to write, write, write.

Chapter 1
The Main Event

I can't imagine why I looked so uncomfortable. Normally my bed was a safe haven for me with cool sheets and nary a wrinkle with a soft mattress that molds to my every curve. This however was nothing like my bed being hot, clammy, and extremely odorous. I was trying to remember the last thing on my mind. Was I working out at the Y? Was I shopping? Was I having coffee in my apartment with our maintenance man, Nick? I couldn't remember. When I tried to move my arm from underneath my body, nothing happened. As I attempted to turn over, my body did not respond to the commands from my brain. I looked around me but could not identify my surroundings. All I knew at this point was that I had ended up in a place I would never expect to be.

I was lying in what looked like a huge steel box that was open at the top with massive amounts of rust running down along the inside walls. When I was finally able to look around, I saw there were black garbage bags piled all around me along with a torn lampshade, a scrap of old carpeting, and a piece of an overstuffed armchair. Without notice, another garbage bag comes crashing down on my head, although I did not feel it.

By the looks of it, I was in a garbage dumpster but where was it located? This was all surreal and I was hoping I would wake up from this horrible nightmare very soon. It seemed so authentic, but it couldn't be. These images must have been caused by the chili I had for dinner last night. That's it! This was all because I ate that spicy chili so close to my bedtime. It happened all the time. I just had to wait for my alarm clock to start screaming which would wake me up. I waited for what seems hours, but was more likely minutes, and the alarm never sounded.

I saw Elaine Swanson putting her garbage bag into the dumpster, including some cardboard that she knew perfectly well should be put into the recycle bins, when she looked over the edge of the dumpster and saw something that must have looked very strange. She looked like she couldn't identify what was lying among the garbage bags, but once her eyes became adjusted to the low light in the trash room she exclaimed, "That looks like a mannequin that someone tossed in the garbage. How strange." But the more she examined my still form, and the more she studied the juxtaposition of the item it became clear to her that she was actually looking at a real human being, not a mannequin.

I heard her screaming very close by. "Ahhhhh, this cannot be happening! someone call 911!" Elaine raced out of the trash room and ran to the office where Linda Carmichael was meeting with a prospective tenant.

"What is the matter, Elaine?"

"Linda, co-co-co-co-come and look. Oh, it is awful! Don't make me go back in there!"

Linda Carmichael, the building manager, didn't have a clue what Elaine was shouting about, but Elaine was sobbing so hard that she could not speak except to utter nonsensical words. And, given the knowledge that Elaine was known for her excitability, Linda didn't know how to identify the problem. She felt like slapping Elaine across the face to bring her out of her hysteria, but that wouldn't do. Finally, after Linda gave Elaine a glass of water and she calmed down enough, Elaine repeated, "It's in the trash room. Do something! Please, do something!"

Linda excused herself, telling the client to please wait in the office, and went down the hall to the trash room. At first, she didn't know where to look, and she saw nothing out of the ordinary. Then she stood on her tiptoes so she could look inside the large steel dumpster, and she froze in place. There was a scream lodged in Linda's throat, but she could not make a sound. It wasn't apparent who was actually lying among the garbage bags because only part of the body was visible, but it really didn't matter right now. Linda felt weak in the knees and almost passed out, but she knew she had to get hold of herself and take control of the situation. The commotion this was going to cause made her stiffen her backbone, stand up straight, and take the steps necessary to get the police involved.

When Linda rushed back to her office and called 911 she could still barely speak. "This is Linda Carmichael at Eden Estates Apartments. We are located at 6204 3rd Street in Margin. There is a person in the dumpster, and I can't tell if they are dead or alive. Please hurry!!"

Linda had experienced second thoughts about accepting this new position, and now she knew why. When she was the manager's assistant, the most trouble she encountered was when someone had wandered away from the building, and she had to go searching for him. He was found down the road at a café enjoying a piece of pie and coffee. He couldn't pay for it of course, because he still had on his pajamas and robe and no money. Linda paid for his food and took him back to the apartment building. Now that she was the building manager, all of the problems, including this crisis, landed in her lap.

The prospective tenant stood up and probably had second thoughts about moving into a place where people, dead or alive, were found in the trash room dumpster. He stammered, "Well, I-I-I think I will come back later. It looks like you have a lot to deal with right now." He dashed out the door as if his pants were on fire. I can just imagine what he would be telling his friends and family why he had changed his mind about moving into Eden Estates.

Linda returned to the trash room and tried to block the door. At least six people were trying to gain entrance as they shouted questions at her like bullets. "What is going on in there? How come you won't let us in? We heard you had called the police, why did you do that?" Evidently Elaine had shared what she had seen with others in the building.

Why did the residents ignore her when Linda told them that the fire department was coming to test the fire alarms and then act surprised when the entire building was filled with very loud sirens. But when she didn't want anyone to know about something like this, the word spread through the halls in a matter of seconds? People came out of their apartments and fled down to the first floor as if Linda was giving away free money.

Linda had to make something up to appease the growing throng. "There is nothing that concerns any of you. You can't do anything here. Just go back to your apartments."

Despite her best efforts, Linda could not hold the people away from the door. Several worked their way around her and rushed into the trash room.

She was hoping that someone would show up soon to help her control the crowd of frightened, hysterical people. Just then Nick Olson, the building's maintenance man, appeared but even he couldn't keep everyone out of the trash room. He wasn't even aware of what had transpired. All he knew was people were filling the 1st floor hallway and looking confused. Linda was not aware that Nick Olson the maintenance man, had arrived so she was trying to get people out of the area all by herself. There were several people peering over the edge of the trash container, and I heard a collective gasp. One woman fainted and others went pale. I feared they were going to vomit right on top of me. Linda and the police officers tried to remove the onlookers and keep everyone else from coming near the box. With all of the pushing and shoving, I was worried that someone could get hurt. Linda was doing her best to move people away from the dumpster so that the emergency people could enter the room.

Soon, they could hear sirens and see flashing lights out the first-floor windows. The first to arrive were police officers including Sgt. Sean Cummings, then the fire department with the EMTs, and then an ambulance. The EMTs moved swiftly down the hall with their equipment. They knew where the problem was due to the fact there were several people around the trash room. They had to shove several people aside in order to enter the room. "Please step aside. Let us pass," an EMT shouted.

Someone yelled, "Let me see what's going on here. I live here too you know. I have a right to know what the fuss is all about."

Another resident said that she knew something was going to happen because her tarot cards told her so just the other day. "The cards never give me wrong information. I could have warned whoever is in the dumpster if they had just asked me for a reading. Everyone knows I have these abilities. I feel so bad that I didn't have the time to warn them. Maybe this is all my fault." She ran away sobbing. I wasn't sure who was speaking. I didn't recognize the voice.

I still was not comfortable with this situation because I had never given much thought about what it would be like to be dead. I had no concrete opinions about an afterlife, but this was nothing like I had expected. I didn't have any memory about who had killed me or why. I couldn't remember anyone doing anything to cause my death, but I was pretty sure I hadn't taken my own life. I couldn't imagine why my spirit had decided to stick around after my body had been removed. All I could verify right now was that I felt no pain, and I liked being able to see everything going on without anyone seeing me.

When Sgt. Cummings entered the building, he looked exactly what my perception of a seasoned cop should looked like — paunchy, balding, bags under his eyes from lack of sleep, and a permanent expression on his face that shouted, "Don't mess with me."

When he had received the call at the station, the only thing he was told was there had been a body found at Eden Estates senior apartment building. "Looks like there may be something more complicated going on here. I'm calling in the ME (Medical Examiner)."

When the ME arrived and examined my body, he noticed that my eyes were wide open and my body was twisted with an arched back and hands like claws. It didn't take long for the ME to realize that this had been no accident because nobody crawls into a filthy dumpster to kill themselves by taking a poison. "I definitely think that this was no accident and that probable cause of death was the ingestion of strychnine." So, it was determined there was definitely a crime involved.

They finally removed my physical body and laid it on the floor. Due to the condition of my body, an arched back and constricted muscles, the ME already had a clue as to what had caused my death but said nothing to the people standing nearby. My remains were then zipped into a large rubber bag that was then placed gently on a gurney. As they were wheeling my body out to the ambulance it dawned on me that my spirit had not joined my earthly form as it was leaving the building, but had chosen to stay behind floating near the ceiling, so I could peer down on the others who were still among the living. I remember thinking, "I am going to find out who killed me if it is the last thing I ever do." Which, of course it would be. I believed this is the reason my spirit was still around. I needed to find my killer.

That was the hardest part of this entire situation. Many people in the building read mystery books, but to have something like this happen for real in their own home was unconscionable. It would certainly make everyone uneasy.

An officer on the CSI team saw Sgt. Cummings walking into the building and said under his breath to a new member of the team, "That is Sean Cummings, and we are lucky that we get to work with him. He has a penchant for being able to see through the bull shit of uncooperative suspects and false evidence. He gets to the heart of the matter in the shortest time possible. He just has an instinct when he looks at crime scenes, and whoever he assigns to this case will have to measure up to his standards or heads will roll. Even though he gives off an aura of sternness, the men and women who work with him respect and admire him."

Sgt. Cummings approached Linda and introduced himself. "Hello, ma'am. I am Sgt. Cummings of the Margin Police department."

Linda then introduced herself saying, "I'm Linda Carmichael, and I am the resident manager of Eden Estates."

Sgt. Cummings tried to reassure Linda when he said, "I want you to know we will do our best to gather what we need and interrupt the people in this building as little as possible. Was the victim a resident in the building?"

Linda nodded. "She was Mrs. Betty Nelson, and she did indeed live here in apartment #340 for over two years."

Speaking to the numerous law enforcement officers on the scene he said, "I need a couple of CSIs to stay here and continue to process this scene and three more to go up to Mrs. Nelson's apartment with me and seal it off. Sam, when you are finished in here, come join me in the victim's apartment. I want you to get photographs of her apartment before it is processed. Since we don't know what took place, or if anyone else was involved, I want all of the i's dotted and the t's crossed."

He returned to Linda and said, "We will need to seal off the trash room and all of the shoots that feed the dumpster until we collect the evidence and clear the scene. Also, the apartment will be off-limits until we can examine that area. We will be collecting all of the trash containers in the building, so I would appreciate it if none of the residents add anything to the them until after we have removed the plastic liners. We will let you know when the trash room is available again, but this will take some time. These officers will remain here until the scene is cleared."

"I know this will be difficult for you Ms. Carmichael, and the residents, but we will need your cooperation to do our investigations. Our main goal will be to find the person or persons who perpetrated this crime."

"Sergeant, do you know how long this will take? Many of the residents are in compromised health situations and this will be very hard on them. Just to know that someone here has died in this building will be very upsetting for them."

Sgt. Cummings told her that he didn't know how long this would take, but they would do their job with as much expediency as possible. The sergeant then went up to my apartment where he found the standard crime scene tape X-ed across the doorway. I followed closely behind him. He took a look around the apartment — closets, cabinets and the kitchen — noticing dishes in the sink and the remainder of apple pie in a tin on the counter top. To me it looked like he wanted to snitch a piece of pie, but he refrained and left the difficult task of collecting evidence to the professionals on his team.

I stayed in the apartment after Sgt Cummings left to watch the process that was being used to collect evidence. One team was gathering up everything in my refrigerator and the dishes in the sink and on the counter. They were very carefully putting each item in an individual evidence bag, writing the date, time and location in which it was found on the bag. Others were spreading fingerprint powder all over door knobs, my computer and mouse, and every surface in the bathroom, bedroom and kitchen. I was glad to know that I would not be responsible for cleaning up this mess. They collected my purse, and someone had gone through my bedroom and bathroom closets and medicine cabinet. If they collected much more in those big plastic bags there would not be anything left for my family to claim when they came for my funeral.

Oh, no. In all of the excitement, I had not even thought about how my family would react when they were told of my death. I was happy that my husband, Larry, was already gone and would not have to deal with any of this.

I floated back downstairs to the office where Linda told the Sergeant that she needed to notify my next of kin as soon as possible. Sgt. Cummings informed her that they would take care of the notification. She looked in my file for my son's name, address, and phone number and turned it over to the Sergeant. Linda was very relieved that she would not have to call my family. At this point Linda broke down. She closed the office door and grabbed a handful of tissues. As she sat in her chair, she sobbed so hard she was shaking.

"How could this happen here?" she asked herself. "How am I going to explain this to the residents? When people move their family members in here, they have an expectation that they will remain safe within these walls. Oh damn. I bet I am going to get a lot of questions from other residents' families about this. I don't know what to tell them." Linda tried to pull herself together so that she could gain the strength to deal with whatever was asked of her. All she knew was that this is not what she signed up for. Just then the phone rang, and Linda was so startled she flew out of her chair with such force that it slammed against the bank of file cabinets on the back wall.

Linda answered with a cautious, "Hello. Who is this?" After a few seconds, she said into the receiver, "No, No. I have nothing to say to your newspaper. Just leave me alone and don't call back."

About 30 minutes later after Sgt. Cummings checked in with both teams of investigators, he returned to Linda's office and told her he would make an announcement to the residents before leaving the building.

"Oh, I think the news will be better received coming from me than you. Some of the people here have a hard time facing reality, and I think I will be able to calm them down."

He said, "Since I don't know what evidence will be discovered, I cannot give you a specific time when all of the officers will vacate the building, but they should not interrupt anything else going on here. There will be investigators here tomorrow to begin the interviews with the staff and residents."

The residents scurried down the hallway to congregate in the community room and await an explanation of why I had been found dead in the trash dumpster of our apartment building. Many of the residents of Eden Estates stayed together long after the ambulance had left to ponder what had taken place in the home where they had all felt so safe, until today that is. Nothing like this had ever happened before, and they were not sure how to cope with this new and frightening situation.

When Linda entered the community room, there were about 30 people sitting around in little groups having coffee and whispering among themselves.

"Can I have your attention everyone?" Linda raised her voice a little. "I know you are all upset, but I have every faith in the Margin Police Department, and I know they will discover exactly what happened here this morning."

"How do you know that? We don't even know what happened, and we live here." Alice was saying what everyone else was thinking. "How did Betty die? It couldn't have been an accident, but the police won't tell us anything."

Linda listened to several people's comments and questions. "They didn't tell me anything either, but when I know something I will share the information."

I didn't understand why this was happening, but I was hoping if I paid close attention it would all make sense to me sooner rather than later. It was interesting watching everyone discuss what had just happened and throwing out suggestions about why this had happened, in of all places, a senior apartment building.

This was the worst Monday morning I could ever remember experiencing. I was also surprised that there were so many people out and about before 9:00 am in the morning.

The residents who I had become friends with in the past two years were crying, wringing their hands, and looking suspiciously at the others in the room. It seemed that the entire population of Eden Estates was crammed into the community room, a space that was normally occupied by five to ten people. It became apparent that the solution to bringing everyone out from their apartments, including those who never graced the others with their presence, was to simply have one of their own murdered.

Soon it became clear to me that the reason my spirit was still in residence was so I could find out why this unfortunate event had happened to me and who did the dirty deed.

I was able to float through walls and floors in order to listen in while people talked with each other in the building and to outsiders on the phone. It was amazing that many of the conversations I was hearing between the residents took on an entirely different dimension when they were speaking to outsiders. Sometimes they would make one statement to a neighbor, but an entirely different one to someone else. Many of the residents phoned friends and relatives and gave radically different stories about what they thought had happened in their building. None of them actually knew what had transpired, yet so they made up stories to make it even more exceptional than it really was.

I heard JoAnn say to one of her friends in the building, "I know it was someone in this building, I just know it." Ten minutes later she was speaking to her aunt on the phone and stated, "Auntie, I am sure that the police will discover this happened when someone from the outside was able to enter the building in the middle of the night and commit this horrendous act. They probably didn't even know Betty or they would have not picked on her. There are a lot of other people here that may have deserved to be killed, but not Betty."

My main goal now was to figure out how to determine what had happened. What methods would I use? Who should I be spying on? My friends or my enemies? I tried to remember any confrontations I had been a part of, and it seems that I had been involved in an inordinate number of altercations with different people ever since I had moved in.

Sometimes my bull headedness got the better of me, but I also was committed to the belief that I was not ever going to stay silent when someone was bullying me or my friends. It took me many years to learn how to stick up for myself, and I am afraid I sometimes took it too far. I was puzzled, however. Was this a vendetta against me? Was I the intended victim or was I just in the wrong place at the wrong time? I could tell that this was going to require all of the tenacity I could muster in order to solve this crime. So, in reality, I was going to have to focus on remembering almost everyone I ever had a problem with, both my friends and others. I needed to make a plan. Let the detective work begin. I continued to wonder how this had happened. I probably had a mental block about this horrendous situation.

Chapter 2
Meeting the Detectives

Sgt. Cummings had assigned Detectives Lindley and Scott to this case. A few days later, Linda received a visit from the Margin Police Department. Detective David Lindley introduced himself as the lead investigator in my case. He then introduced Detective Sandra Scott and assured Linda that they would do everything possible to determine who was responsible for my untimely death. Linda asked Detective Lindley if they knew the cause of death.

"I am sorry, but I cannot divulge anything related to this ongoing investigation at this point." he answered.

Detective Scott told Linda, "We will be in and out of the building questioning the staff and residents to help us determine who did this and why. We would appreciate everyone's cooperation in our investigation."

Linda was taken aback. "You do realize that this incident has been very upsetting to everyone here, and some people may be reluctant to share what they know if they thought they could get in trouble with you or someone in the building? Since we don't know what happened, or who was involved, they are walking around suspecting everyone they see, even though they may have known each other for many years. Some are feeling that they may be in danger themselves and don't know who to trust. This whole situation has been very difficult for them."

"I understand the delicate nature of this event," stated Detective Lindley. "And that older people can sometimes be unnecessarily worried about talking to the police, but I hope we will be able to count on your help in convincing the residents that our only goal is to find the person responsible and to bring them to justice. I know they have placed crime scene tape across Mrs. Nelson's apartment door, and you need to leave everything as it is. There will be Crime Scene Investigators working in the apartment and public areas again today."

Linda assured the detective that she would cooperate in any way possible and try to convince everybody else to do the same. She wrote a note to put on each apartment door stating what she expected of everyone during this very hard time. She also posted one in the elevator and on the bulletin board by the mail boxes. These were traditionally where people would find a notice about happenings in the building.

Naturally, this was the only topic of conversation in the entire building. Everyone had their own ideas of why this had happened and who was the guilty party.

Chapter 3
The Final Goodbye

It was an extremely strange situation, attending my own funeral, but I thought I may hear something that could help me in my quest for answers. Who would attend, and who would be absent? What would they say about me? Would anyone drop a clue I could use in my quest for answers to the questions I had about my death? I looked marvelous, even better than when blood was coursing through my veins, in fact. The hairstyle was much more modern than how I had worn it in life, and I wish I had tried styling it that way when it mattered. My fingernails were perfectly manicured and donned a subtle shade of pink, a much subtler shade than the red I had normally worn. Some of the jewelry I was wearing were pieces I hadn't seen in years but really complemented my blue dress with the little white collar. I had taken to using much more color in my wardrobe since my husband died, but the subdued presentation probably represented the real me much more honestly. My family had done a wonderful job in choosing what I would be seen in for the last time. I just hope they would remember to remove my jewelry before they shoved me into the big furnace.

Why was it that most people never said nice things about me until I was lying in a satin lined box waiting to be buried or burned? I have to say I was also guilty of this when I went to funerals. I never knew what to say in order to help ease the pain of the bereaved. What could I possibly say that would make any difference to the ones left behind to pick up the pieces after a loved one's life had been extinguished?

My oldest cousin, Olive, was helped up to the lectern by her husband as her cane was not always reliable in unfamiliar spaces. Olive spoke in a small and somewhat shaky voice, "Betty was a very good cook and an excellent baker. I always looked forward to a call from her which usually concluded in an invitation to dinner and an evening of bridge with her and Larry. Betty made us feel at home, and it was nice to be entertained in her dining room where the table was dressed in a linen tablecloth and napkins which had been folded in any number of ingenious ways and placed on her china plates just waiting for the delicious food she had prepared. I never thanked her for all the work she had gone to in order to have us to dinner. I could have brought her flowers or offered to supply dessert, but I never did. She had a very big heart. I love her and will really miss her."

My daughter, Susan, said some very nice things about me also. "I remember when I was in Girl Scouts, and we had the annual camping trip coming the last weekend of June. All eight girls were looking forward to this outing, and we were set to leave for the campground on Friday afternoon. Mom received a phone call from our scout leader saying that she was sick and would need to cancel the trip. I begged Mom to fill in for the scout leader and take us instead. After she received several calls from the other girl's moms, she finally acquiesced and said she would fill in, just this time. There were two other women who had been involved from the very beginning of the planning, so mom didn't need to buy anything or come up with projects. All she had to do was pack her own camping gear and pick up two girls on our way to the campsite. When we arrived at our destination, all of the mothers helped the girls set up the tents and gather wood for the fire that we would keep burning until we left on Sunday afternoon. At least that was the plan."

"After we cooked our HO-BO dinners over the fire and filled our stomachs with 's'mores, we all snuggled into our tents and told ghost stories until mom promised to take us home if we didn't settle down and get some sleep. Within three hours the sky became threatening and a sudden cloudburst turned our campsite into a huge mud puddle. All of us were frightened and running around outside because there was three inches of water in our tents. Mom calmly told us to grab our blankets, and we would all get into the cars where the mothers could run the heater to warm us up and dry our pajama legs. I remember feeling so proud of my mom for coming up with a solution that was simple and kept all of us feeling safe and comfortable. That is just what my mom was like. She'd say that she would put her thinking a cap on, and she always came up with a solution."

Susan said she also appreciated how I helped with her sewing projects in junior high and held her when she was sobbing about her break up with a boy she had been going steady with for two months in the 8th grade.

My son, Robert was not as eloquent as his sister but he also spoke about how he knew I would always be available to talk over problems and not make light about issues that seemed life changing to him at the time. He said, "I will really miss the Russian Teacakes Mom made at Christmas time. My wife has made some, but they just weren't the same as Mom's."

"I also like to think about the time when Mom said she was going to teach me how to swim when I was about five years old. We went down to the lake near our house and entered the water where it was about two feet deep. I remember being very frightened because when my dad had tried to teach me to swim, he tossed me off the end of the dock and expected I would just learn to keep afloat. I dropped to the lake bottom and thought I was going to die. Mom rushed into the water and brought me to shore. Mom's idea was a lot kinder and successful. She held me across her arms in the shallow water and taught me to kick my feet and use my arms. She didn't let go until I told her I felt safe in trying it myself."

If I could have cried, I would have just listening to the wonderful things people said about me.

I had attended St. John's Lutheran Church since I had moved here, and I knew Reverend Stall very well. I talked to him several times during my grieving process when Larry died, and he walked the walk with me until I could stand on my own two feet again. He shared at my funeral that I was an avid volunteer and could be called upon to step in whenever I was needed. Reverend Stall and his wife invited me to dinner several times, and we enjoyed playing bridge with their daughter filling in as my partner. They got to know me not only as a parishioner but as a person. He said some very kind things about me, and I appreciated his eulogy enormously.

There were many flower memorials lined up beside my casket, and I enjoyed floating around reading the sympathy cards attached. Some came from expected sources like my children and other family members. My friends from Eden Estates sent a beautiful spray with a ribbon saying, "Our Good Friend." Several friends from Iowa came for the show and undoubtedly were checking out the people in attendance from Eden Estates. I used to relate to them all of the goings on in our weekly phone calls and emails. I had stayed connected to many of the people from my past as I could always count on them to cheer me up when I felt I was going crazy in the asylum I had called "home" since moving to Wisconsin.

There was one, however, that carried an ominous message. The card simply stated, "Payback." I was shocked and wondered who had sent this mysterious bouquet. I hoped the police officers who attended my funeral took note of the cards and would try to find out who sent them. I would also try to find out in the weeks ahead because it may be a clue to the person responsible for my untimely death.

My only regret was I would have enjoyed many of the compliments and lovely things they were saying about me while I was still alive.

After the funeral, there was of course the obligatory luncheon consisting of macaroni salad, green Jello, a meat and cheese tray, dinner rolls and brownies that had been left out in the air too long. No one returned for a second cup of coffee because they said it tasted like dishwater. But, as far as I remembered, all of this was to be expected at most funeral luncheons, at least Lutheran ones. . .

During the luncheon, my son and daughter were required to listen to several people go on and on about every memory they had of me for the past several years. The ones who had made the trip up from Iowa for the services said some very nice things about me also. It was great for me to be able to attend this final gettogether, in spirit form of course, and I felt so much better hearing they were all startled to find out my death was not at all natural. That fact alone led to some interesting conversations and speculations.

Chapter 4
Gathering the Goods

When everyone finally left the church basement, my son and daughter returned to my apartment and started planning how they would clear everything out before the end of the month so they would not be required to pay an additional month's rent. The police had gathered the evidence they needed and released the apartment back to Linda. It was good to see the crime scene tape had been removed. I had forgotten that I made them copies of my keys when I moved here — just in case of an emergency. Now I was happy I did this because they could come and go anytime they wanted and not have to wait for the manager to be present to let them in.

Any time a person has lived a long life, there are many things collected over the years that gave their life meaning and contributed to their happiness. I was no exception.

My children, started going through my belongings in a haphazard attempt to decide what to do with everything I owned. I am sure it was overwhelming for them. Since I had not expected to be dead, I hadn't picked up the newspapers, vacuumed the carpet, or cleaned the bathroom for several days. If I was alive, I would have been embarrassed for my children to see my home in such disarray. They probably thought I was a pig, but seeing my apartment in this state didn't seem to faze them at all including the fingerprint powder that was on so many surfaces.

Susan found my jewelry box on my bedroom dresser and took it out to the living room so she could spread everything out on the coffee table in order to examine each piece carefully. Granted, I hadn't owned many expensive pieces because my husband had thought spending money on jewelry, flowers, or perfume was a waste of money. I had some rings and bracelets that had belonged to my mother and grandmother that held many wonderful memories for me, and I would be happy for Susan to carry on the tradition of wearing them for special occasions. However, she had other ideas about what pieces were valuable or important.

"Look at all of this junky stuff. I know Mom loved it, but none of these pieces are real gemstones or even 18 carat gold. I wouldn't wear these abominations to the grocery store. Do you want any of this or should I just toss all if it? The only thing worth a plug nickel was her wedding ring. Maybe I will take that and have it made into a pendent necklace. It isn't even a whole carat so it won't be very flashy but at least we shouldn't throw it away."

"I don't want most of what I am seeing," said Robert. "I can't believe she paid someone to move all of this old, broken down furniture from Iowa. This has got to be 30 years old. Can you believe that people thought sofas and chairs with flowers all over them were attractive? I hated this stuff when I was a kid, and I still do. I remember being embarrassed when the furniture store delivered it, even though all their friends were buying the same kind of furniture at the time. I am not sure how we will get rid of it though. We will probably need to pay someone to take it away. Overstuffed furniture is hard to dispose of so maybe we should call one of those places that take anything for a price. I think I will phone the place called, WE LOVE YOUR JUNK tomorrow and set up a time for them to haul away anything we don't want."

If I had been alive, I would have kicked them out of my apartment. I was livid the way they were talking about my beloved possessions. No respect. No sentimentality. No feelings for what I held dear.

Susan started going through my kitchen cabinets and drawers and came to the same conclusion about my things there. "We should be able to pack it all up and give it to a thrift store. I am going to look in the bedroom to see if there is anything we can save, sell, or give away."

Robert was looking at all my treasures in the china cabinet. I had some of those items since I was a child. There were also items Larry and I had gotten for wedding gifts or on vacations, and art projects that were created for me by both my children and grandchildren. Robert picked up a silver cup and spoon my grandmother gave to him when he was born. She said it had been hers as a baby and wanted the good luck it held for her to be passed down to her first great-grandchild. I am sure it had very little monetary value, but I loved it and kept it polished year after year.

Since I had told Robert this story when he was a small boy, he knew how special it was to me. "I am taking this cup home so it will stay in the family." Robert looked sad for the first time since my death. Up to this point, he had just been numb. Ever since the police told him about my death, he had walked around in a daze. If someone had asked me what I saw on his face, it would have been confusion and anger. He was softening. This was good because he needed to let the pain in which meant he could start to grieve.

Robert looked at each figurine, keepsake, and dish in the cabinet. After only about 10 minutes, he looked at Susan and said, "I don't want anything else in here, so after you choose what you want, we can pack up the rest and give it to Goodwill."

Susan glanced in the cabinet and shrugged her shoulders. "I can't see anything I would want out of there. Let's just get some boxes and get rid of all of it."

I was so hurt. My entire life was represented in those items, and they were treating them like trash. Did they always think that of my belongings when they came to visit me? If I could have, I would have cried.

Just then there was a knock on my door. When Robert opened it, there were several friends of mine standing on the threshold. Julie Reynolds, a friend from Iowa, spoke up for the group, "We don't mean to interrupt you in this time of grief, but we are returning to Anthony Falls tomorrow and wanted to know if we could have something that belonged to Betty as a memento, you know."

Robert invited them into the apartment, and there were introductions all around. Susan asked if they had any idea of what they would like to take home with them.

One of the woman said, "If you wouldn't mind I would really like to go through Betty's jewelry. She had some lovely pieces that she wore frequently, and if I could have a piece or two, it would mean a lot to me."

"I was just going through her jewelry and would feel honored if you would take what you would like," Susan offered.

"Oh, are you sure?" asked Julie.

"Yes, I am positive. And if you would like to look around to see if there is anything else you would like, please help yourselves."

Robert offered to show them my treasures in the china cabinet. The women gathered around and started making comments about many of the displayed items.

"Oh, there is the Vaseline glass lemonade pitcher that belonged to her grandmother. Remember? She would use it in the summer to serve lemonade out on the patio in those beautiful green glasses."

"And remember when she would serve us cookies on that plate that her son made in junior-high school? We would laugh about it not being very flat so it would rock back and forth when we took the cookies off it. We all thought it was god-awful ugly, but Betty was so proud of it we had to keep our feelings to ourselves. I would love to have that if you don't want it, Robert."

"No, that is just fine. I would like someone that will appreciate it to have it."

All the women saw something in the jewelry box and china cabinet that they wanted to take back to Iowa.

Susan invited them to look all around the apartment to see what else they might want. By the time they had been through the kitchen, bedroom and walk-in closet, they had collected several things that seemed very important to them. They even chose items for people who weren't there. Nancy stated, "I know some other people would like an item from Betty's personal life also." I was awe struck. I felt so much better knowing my friends would enjoy using my treasures.

They said they would collect several boxes and return the next morning to pack them up before they drove back to Iowa. Susan and Robert were thrilled that they may not have to do as much work they had expected when they first entered my apartment.

"Maybe this won't be as bad as we thought."

Shortly after the women from Iowa had left, there was another knock on the door. Robert was getting annoyed at all the people who had been interrupting the process he and Susan were involved in. Reluctantly, he opened the door. There were six women he recognized from the funeral standing in the doorway, but these people all lived in the building. Like my friends from Iowa they also wanted to know if they could come in and find a treasure of mine they could have. They not only wanted a memento of mine, but also wanted a lot of the furniture. I was thinking that some of them didn't really care about having anything that I owned as much as the opportunity to feather their nests with my old chairs and such.

Tootsie was interested in my china cabinet. JoAnn wanted the dressers in the bedroom and several outfits, if possible. JoAnn thought the sofa and loveseat would be much nicer in her apartment than her present furniture. And she also wanted to know if my china would be available along with my depression glass serving dishes.

After several women had pawed their way through my apartment, there wasn't a whole lot left that Robert and Susan would need to deal with. Things were looking up for all concerned, except me, of course.

None of this had given me any clues as to who would like to kill me. I couldn't believe anyone would plan to murder me just to gain access to my old furniture or wedding china. There had to be a more substantial reason why I was dead. I needed to think back to moments in my life that would lead someone to believe their life would be greatly improved if I were no longer around. It was hurtful to admit there were people that I had hurt, embarrassed, or used to the point that they were willing to take the chance of committing an act that could possibly put them in prison for the rest of their life. I assumed that the perpetrator was someone living at Eden Estates, the senior housing building where I had lived for the past two years, but maybe not.

CHAPTER 5
Before Eden Estates

I remember being a tad nervous when I first moved into Eden Estates in Margin, WI a few months after my husband died. He had been fighting cancer for several years and finally succumbed to that terrible disease. I was very worried about where I was going to live. I lacked the funds to rent a market value apartment, even in Iowa. My friends did all they could for me, but I wasn't at all comfortable taking what I would consider "charity." I knew my life was going to change, I just didn't know how much.

My son had approached me about moving to an affordable senior apartment building in Margin so I could be near him, his sister and their families.

"Mom," Robert said." I think you would be very happy here. Your family is all here in Wisconsin, and it is a very nice place to live. We are a lot bigger than Anthony Falls, and we have all the conveniences of a bigger city. You won't be living right in the city of course but on the north side where Sherrie and I live. We have a wonderful hospital, and you know we have great parks because we have gone there with the kids when you and Dad visited us. We have a YMCA very close, and they offer all kinds of classes you might like. I have been investigating the possibilities of affordable housing and there are many places that have a sliding rent scales where they only required you to pay 30% of your monthly income for rent. There is one place that both Susan and I like very much, and they have some immediate openings. If you would like me to, I can fill out an application for you. I would be happy to do that, and you could probably move in very soon. What do you say?"

I wasn't at all sure that I wanted to leave my home and friends, but I also didn't see any other option. I thought I may as well move to Wisconsin because then I would at least be near my children and grandchildren. After much soul searching, I called my son and said, "I would like to take you up on your offer to find me a place to live in Wisconsin."

He called me back a few days later and said I could be in the new apartment in two months. He even sent me some pictures of the building and my future apartment. The building was four stories with a brick exterior and a covered patio on the East side. The apartment was small, really small — about 500 square feet — but it would be just fine after I got rid of everything I didn't need. I knew this move would be hard, but I was determined to make it work.

I was worried about selling my home in Iowa, but my attorney said if it hadn't sold by the time I was ready to move, he would act on my behalf and take care of it for me. Luckily, the first couple who looked at it fell in love with the house and gardens I had worked in for 40 years. They could see how much work Larry and I had put into keeping the house updated. The gardens were like a mini park with paths to walk and a bench near the koi pond which made it a very peaceful spot to meditate or pray. They made me a full-price offer which I readily accepted.

Larry and I had lived in our house for about 40 years, so I knew we had more possessions than I would ever need to take to my new home. As I started cleaning out the closets, many of my good friends offered to help me. I had met Doreen and Peter shortly after we had moved to this house in Anthony Falls. She was my best friend and knew more about me than another person on earth. I was glad she was going to join me in my sorting because she would understand what I was attached to and what I was willing to donate or sell at a garage sale.

Doreen appeared at my door the next morning with two large cups of coffee and two bear claw pastries from the café down the street. She knew me well. We seated ourselves at the kitchen table where we had shared thousands of cups of coffee and spilled our guts out to each other through the years. We helped our children with their algebra, built science projects, and made cookies here for our daughters when they were trying to earn a cooking badge for their Girl Scout sash.

When we finished our coffee, we went to the basement and into a storage room I had not entered in probably five years. When Larry was struggling with his cancer, not much was accomplished around my house except the basic cooking and cleaning, so I knew I would find things in this room I hadn't even thought about in a very long time.

I found boxes of the children's school papers, awards and papier-mâché volcanoes stored in the basement. Doreen asked me, "Do Robert and Susan know you still have all of this junk in your basement that belongs to them?"

"Well, probably not to the extreme that I have here," I answered.

"I think you should get one of those big containers where you can put anything you don't want to keep or sell, and then the company comes back to get it and takes it all away."

"I guess you are right, Doreen, and I really need your help, but I think we need more help than just you and me. It would take us six months to go through it, and I don't have that much time."

"How about if I call the girls and set a date for them to come here to help. If we had all six of us working on this, we could accomplish a lot in a short period of time."

"OK, you call Alice and Ruth, and I'll call Carolyn and Lynn." We had all grown up together and had kept in touch all these years so I felt strongly that they would be happy to help me in my hour of need.

That weekend five women, dressed in the clothes we call our grubbies, showed up at my house at 8:00 am and started to pitch in. I had given them all a tour of the house, including the attic, basement, and garage and told them what I wanted to get rid of and what I would need to go through myself. I had ordered a dumpster, and it started to fill up fast. I told them any clothes of Larry's could go because I had no energy to sort through the items that still held his distinctive scent.

I couldn't believe how much we pulled out of nooks and crannies. Carolyn said, "I can't believe you still have things we had in high school. Your cheerleader outfit, the tent we used to go camping, old pictures of people that we don't even know anymore. Why did you keep all of this?"

"I think I had a hard time getting rid of these and many other items, because it was a sign that I was growing older even though I haven't looked at it in years, I knew it was still around. OK, call me a hoarder. I have known for years that I should have gotten rid of most of the old, unusable items but it became so overwhelming I didn't know how or where to start. I am so ashamed of myself."

Carolyn came over and gave me a long, warm hug while I cried until I couldn't breathe.

"Come sit down, Betty. You don't have to feel that way. I also have lots of old, unnecessary stuff. But, Betty, this is a brand new start for you, and you have the opportunity to decide what is really important and what at this point in your life holds no meaning for you. I am willing to stay here and help you go through every closet, drawer, and cubby hole until you only have the items left that you want to sell or give away or take to your new home. I'll bet the others would pitch in too, and we could maybe even have fun with some of the things we will discover. We all love you and none of us will tell a living soul about what we find."

"All right, let's pull together and get this done," I agreed.

The six of us spent the entire weekend opening boxes and bags and tossing them into the dumpster. While I was carrying a box of old greeting cards out to the dumpster, I saw Lynn and Alice in the driveway trying to use hula-hoops without much success. Their bodies just didn't want to move the way they did when they were 10 years old. I was laughing so hard I thought I would pee my pants.

"Hey, you two! You are supposed to be throwing all of that stuff out, not play with it."

"We, know," said Lynn. "We just wanted to see if we could still do it. Obviously, you are not the only one living in the past."

It was getting late in the afternoon, and we had worked so hard we had all but cleaned out the basement and garage of unwanted items. We decided to call it a day. They all said they would be back the next day, and Lynn said she would bring her husband Rob to lift the heavy things into the dumpster. I was exhausted so I took a long hot bath and fell asleep on the sofa by 10:00pm.

The next day we cleaned out the attic and finished the basement. I don't know what I would have done without my friends. They put the things I wanted for the sale in the garage, and the trash was removed. I felt so much better.

"I don't know how to thank all of you. I could have never done this by myself."

"Betty, we will be here again next weekend to help with the sale and take the rest of the items that are worth anything to the thrift store."

I thought to myself, "How am I going to find friends like this is Wisconsin? This was why I was dragging my feet about selling my house and moving. It took me almost all of my life to create friendships like the ones I had here. Our kids went to the same schools, most of us attended the same church, and our husbands went golfing and hosted barbeques together."

After I paid off all of Larry's medical bills, I had very little money left from the sale of the house, and I felt better knowing that I would not have to spend my entire social security check to pay rent in the new apartment.

So, I packed up and relocated to Margin, WI, but I knew I would still miss my home and friends in Anthony Falls. If it hadn't been for my husband's lingering illness, I would still be living in my own home, tending my garden, and sewing new curtains for the guest room. I knew my children were right convincing me to move near them at this stage of my life, but I was already homesick.

My son, Robert, and his wife Sherrie lived about five miles from my new residence, and he assured me he and his family would see me often if I moved to Margin. However, since Robert traveled a lot for his job and Sherrie owned her own small business, I knew there wouldn't be as many Sunday dinners together as I was led to believe.

Susan and Anthony Cousins, my daughter and son-in-law, lived about 15 miles away from me in a small town. The owned a small farm with crops and animals that needed almost constant attention. So, again, I would not be spending much time with them either. I had two grandsons and three granddaughters ranging in age from five to 19 years of age. If I wanted to see them, I had to make an appointment with their parents so they would be at home when I arrived or hope the older kids would take time out of their very busy social lives to see their old grandma. Since I had lived in Iowa all of their lives and only saw them on occasional family vacations, I did not have a close personal relationship with any of them. I was hoping to change all of that when I moved to Margin. In fact, thinking of spending more time with my kids and grandchildren was a major determining factor when I was thinking of moving after Larry died. I was, however, having second thoughts about what I had just done. Was I really ready to start all over in new town, in a new state where the only people I knew were mostly absent from my life? I hated the thought of trying to make new friends and learn where everything was located in my new city. However, if I was ever going to feel like this was my home, I would have to venture out on my own.

Even though I was not nearly done with my unpacking, I was anxious to start finding my way around. First, I decided to find a grocery store. My cabinets and refrigerator needed to be filled, and I wanted to be able to cook my own meals. I had been in my new apartment for three days and had eaten out every day. This was not only bad for my waistline, but also my pocketbook.

I decided to call my daughter for some help. "Susan, can you tell me the best place to buy groceries?" I asked.

"Oh, Mom, I think you would like Freddy's Grocery Store. It is only about one mile from you and will have everything you need. The prices are not too bad either. Just buy what you will need until the weekend because then Tony and I will take you to the warehouse store that is about ten miles away. You won't need a membership because we can just add you to ours. That way, you can go there anytime you want to with or without us. You will be able to stock up on paper products and frozen food. But for right now, I think Freddy's would be your best choice."

After Susan gave me directions from my apartment to the grocery store, I felt like I was finally on my own. As I drove to the grocery store I noticed that there was a pharmacy, beauty salon, and dry cleaner in the strip mall attached to Freddy's Grocery Store along with a Chinese restaurant and a gas station. I was so happy to know that these services were so close to my new home.

I normally find it hard to find my way around a store that is unfamiliar to me, however, Freddy's Grocery Store was laid out in a very customer friendly manner. The aisles were clearly marked and very wide. There also happened to be a coffee shop right in the store which I took advantage of when I needed a break from shopping. After loading my groceries into my car, I drove adjacent to the sidewalk to see what else was in the mall: a minute clinic, greeting card store, and discount store were all places I could see myself patronizing.

As I drove home, I felt much better about where I was living and was beginning to feel more at home already. It was nice having my children close, but I wanted to be as independent as possible.

One of the things I was concerned about was taking a driving test for a Wisconsin driver's license. I had never taken a driver's test before because when I received my Iowa license all that was required was that I send in $10 to the state, and they issued me a license without me ever proving I could actually operate a motor vehicle. So, when the day came for my test, a very young, sober looking instructor climbed into the passenger side of my car. I felt I was doomed to taking public transportation from now on. However, I passed with a 100% and went home feeling I had received a reprieve for several more years.

I am an intelligent woman, and I know we all get old eventually, but when I awoke one morning and found my 68-year-old body struggling to get out of bed, I was genuinely surprised. I had been very active all my life and enjoyed activities like walking, biking, and attending concerts. However, I had also enjoyed more adventurous activities like ballroom dancing, skiing, and SCUBA diving. But due to my current situation, I was afraid that they were all a thing of the past. I just couldn't afford those types of activities now, but I was a firm believer that if I didn't use my muscles and mind, they would melt away like a bowl of ice cream left out in the sun too long. I looked at this new lifestyle as an adventure and fully expected to take advantage of all that Margin had to offer.

I immersed myself in unpacking the many boxes I had convinced myself I couldn't live without when packing in Iowa. Although, I wasn't sure how a 30-cup coffee maker would be used (or stored) in my small apartment with very little storage space. As I continued to empty the boxes, it occurred to me that my children had been correct in trying to convince me I wouldn't need two dozen wine glasses, three sets of china, plus everyday dishes. Or the many electrical cords I still had after the appliances they belonged to had been given to Goodwill years ago. I didn't want to face the fact, but it became clear, that I was a packrat. Living in the same house for 40 years, with several closets, a full basement, and a two-car garage allowed me to hang onto things I didn't need or want. I hated to think of the money I wasted paying movers to pack up and move all of the boxes full of items I would end up giving to charity or throwing away.

    Well, this was about to change. I wanted to be comfortable here and holding on to boxes of "stuff" I would never use again was not on the agenda. My surprise at finding all of this junk really surprised me because I thought I had gotten rid of the minutiae in my house before I sold it. I found out where the thrift stores were located and donate most of the things I still needed to unpack. I would simply open a box, remove right then and there what I would keep, put it where it belonged in this new space, close the box, and move it to an empty corner of the apartment. Once I had a plan I felt much better but I was exhausted just thinking of the task ahead. I decided to check out the community room where it seemed everyone congregated for coffee and socializing. I had heard it described as the "lifeblood" of the building, so I was excited to experience what everyone else thought was so important.

Chapter 6
My First Impression

My first impression as I entered the community room was, "Everyone here is so old." I was probably one of the youngest residents in the building, but still, these people looked like they all had one foot in the grave. I could see the writing on the wall. I would be pushing people around in wheelchairs and helping them across the road to the strip mall where they did most of their shopping. I was beginning to think I made a rash decision in moving here.

I took my first look around the community room. It was about 40 feet long and 20 feet wide. The walls were the same as every other public space in the building with oatmeal colored walls, newer carpeting consisting of several shades of browns and windows on the three exterior walls. It had a small kitchen that looked well equipped. I was told before I moved in occasional potluck dinners were held here and the coffee pot was always on. Evidently, several residents took turns making coffee so that duty did not fall to only one person. Good to know.

All of a sudden, I heard a loud, raspy voice. "There is a time and a place for everything, and this is not the time or the place for what I just saw out by the mailboxes," Alice Ready stated boldly as she poured herself a cup of coffee and took a seat next to a frail looking woman I learned later to be Jennifer Arensen.

"What's going on?" asked another woman at the same table as she put her knitting down in her lap.

"I just saw Janice kissing a man on the lips, in the foyer, right out in front of everyone," replied Alice. "Can you imagine her being so brazen?"

Jennifer spoke up to defend Janice Tuthill, "That was Janice's son who is visiting here from New York. There is nothing wrong with a son kissing his mother. Bruce only gets to see Janice a couple of times a year, and I think it is wonderful that he is so affectionate with his mother. Alice, you are just jealous because your kids rarely come to see you, even though they only live 20 minutes from here. And I have never seen them be so affectionate with you even when they do visit."

Alice squirmed in her seat but did not back down from what she had said. After all, she knew she was never wrong.

I had a feeling I would learn everything I needed to know about Eden Estates sitting right here in this community room. It became obvious this was indeed the nerve center of the building, and I would take advantage of that little fact.

I helped myself to coffee and sat at a table close to the others where I could listen in, but not look like I was eavesdropping. When another resident entered the room, she came right over to my table and asked if I minded her sitting with me.

"No, please sit down," I said. I introduced myself, "I am Betty Nelson, and I just moved here from Anthony Falls, Iowa."

The other woman introduce herself, "I am Tootsie Zacaris, and I have lived here for eight years so I can help you find everything you need here in Margin. If you are interested, we can have fun exploring the shopping areas and restaurants. I moved in here after my husband died of a heart attack, and when he was gone, I realized Ron had been in charge of everything around the house and I just couldn't keep it up by myself any longer. I thought I was going to stay in the house we had shared for 45 years and where we raised our four children, but I just couldn't afford it. We had taken out a home improvement loan and done extensive remodeling to our home, but we hardly started paying the bank back when Ron died. I had to sell it, and after paying off the loan, I didn't have very much money left. Welcome to Eden Estates."

I said, "I am unfamiliar with anyone or anything around here except my daughter and son who live close by. They are the ones who convinced me to move here. They both have jobs and my grandchildren are always busy too, so I am sort of on my own trying to find my way around."

I felt very comfortable with Tootsie as she shared more. "My only sister lives in California. She said I could go live with her but I was used to living in the mid-west and never gave a thought to moving to the west coast. Eden Estates is a nice place to live. I think you will like it here, at least most of the time." Tootsie was a little slip of a woman with curly brown hair that looked like she had just come from the beauty salon, but she assured me it was just naturally easy to style. She said she was 78, but she didn't look a day over 68, my own age.

Tootsie and I sat and chatted for a while, but when the mail carrier entered the building, there was a mass exodus as everyone moved into the foyer where the mailboxes were located. It was like watching a cattle drive. People who looked like they could not leave their chairs unassisted rushed out of the room like they were 30 years old. Tootsie said, "This is the highlight of the day for many of the people here. They will rush to open their boxes and then sit and compare what each of them has been endowed with today. I don't know anywhere else where junk mail is read thoroughly and discussed at length. If someone gets a catalogue that the others didn't receive, there is jealousy among the ranks. When anyone has received a personal letter or card, it is passed among the others after the owner has committed it to memory."

One of the women had received a fat envelope that looked very official and across the front in large print stated," YOU HAVE WON THE FANTASTIC MAGAZINE CONTEST." JoAnn Teaness squealed and waved the envelope in the air. "I can't believe it, I don't even remember entering the contest." All of a sudden, she looked worried and sat down heavily in the closest chair.

"What's the matter, JoAnn?" asked Lorraine Story. JoAnn had opened the envelope and was reading all about her good fortune, but she looked worried. "If I have won this money," she whispered," I will need to move out of this apartment. They don't allow wealthy people to live in affordable housing buildings." JoAnn started weeping into her handkerchief and hyperventilating. Everyone was concerned and tried to calm her down. "I don't want to move away from all of my friends and my home here." JoAnn stuttered through her sobs adding, "I have to go home and think about this." I had been told that JoAnn was a very excitable person in her everyday life, so something like this put her over the edge of reason.

No one had the heart to tell her that millions of people had received the same letters and none of them had won anything. Evidently, JoAnn had received several of these letters throughout the years, and she always fell for the same ploy. Behind her back, most people felt bad for her but also laughed at her gullibility.

Tootsie and I waited for the foyer to empty before we went to our mailboxes and removed the junk mail we both received. We looked at each other and laughed. I had a feeling that Tootsie and I would become friends.

I went back to my apartment and put my new plan to work. I opened several boxes, and after removing the items I could actually use, taped them back up and piled the boxes in the corner. After four hours I decided I needed a break. This process was both mentally and physically exhausting. However, I did feel good sorting through the boxes and eliminating what I didn't need that someone else could use. I even found some furniture pieces that really didn't fit into my new space, and I was sure that someone could tell me a place that could use a table or two, a tall bookcase, and a dining room table with four chairs.

My son sent me the dimensions of my rooms and several pictures of my apartment before I even left Iowa, but somehow it was a lot smaller than I had expected. Given the placement of the windows and air conditioner, my furniture was limited to one configuration. The cable for the TV and computer was located on the long wall as I walked into the apartment, so that was the only place to put my electronics. I was used to having much more space where I could rearrange the furniture and throw rugs any time I became bored with it. This was going to take some getting used to.

However, this was just one more thing I was going to need to come to grips with. Over were the days when I could buy whatever I wanted and travel whenever the mood grabbed me. The decision to move on with my life was completely up to me. I felt a little depressed about all of the changes to my life, and I was still grieving not only the loss of my husband but the loss of a lifestyle I had enjoyed for many years. It was disconcerting realizing everything in my life had changed, and I either had to change my attitude or be miserable. I hoped I would meet some people I could call friends and get to know on a personal level, not just a superficial one.

Back to the community room I went. In the hallway, a very determined woman came up to me and without so much as a "hello" said, "Do you drive?"

"Yes," I replied.

"Do you own a car?"

"Yes, I do. Why?"

"Well, you can't park in any of those spaces in front of the building. They are reserved for certain other people," she stated.

"Oh, are they handicapped spaces?" I guessed.

She looked me right in the eye and said, "No, they aren't. But some of us have been parking there for many years, and no one else is allowed to park there."

Just then another woman named Elaine approached us and said, "Marianne, it states in the resident handbook, and Linda just told Betty, that there are no reserved spaces except the handicapped ones."

I could see Marianne turn an ugly shade of purple when she said through clenched teeth, "I don't care what she was told. If she parks in the wrong place, she will not be happy with the consequences." I had just met Marianne Taylor, the building bully.

I was wondering, if I parked in the "wrong place" would I come out of the building and find nails in my tires or a have a broken headlight? It seemed that this was a much tougher crowd than I had expected.

I turned to Marianne and said as politely as I could muster, "I have been parking down by the north doorway because my apartment is right up the stairs, so I just have to run up the stairs, and I am home."

Marianne just glared at me and said, "Oh, you're one of them. You can run up the stairs so you think you are better than the rest of us." She abruptly turned and left the room.

Genevieve Carlson rolled her eyes and asked me if I would like to join her for coffee. We proceeded to the community room at a slow sprint. Little did I know there was a plethora of unwritten rules in this place.

Genevieve seemed very friendly, but spoke in a hushed tone, as if someone was listening to our conversation as we visited over coffee. She had short blond hair and the bluest of eyes that twinkled in the sunlight coming through the window. "I haven't lived here very long myself, but I do know there are many shopping and dining options not far from here. I am originally from Margin so the biggest reason I moved here is because the rent is so reasonable. My family lives nearby so I often get to see my children and grandchildren. I actually drive my granddaughter to school every day so she can attend a college prep high school instead of the neighborhood school that is just not as challenging. My grandson is in his first year of college and lives on campus, but we meet for lunch a couple of times a month. I have been so lucky to live near my family all the time my grandchildren have been around, so I have a great relationship with all of them. I feel sorry for those who don't have family close or never get to see them. If you are interested, there are a lot of things for seniors to do around here so you will only need to be bored if that is your choice."

I was happy to have met Genevieve, and I thought we could have some fun together too. Most of the people I met were very nice and told me if I needed anything I could call on them. Which is what most people say when someone new moves into building, where everyone else knows each other. It would become clear, very soon who I could really count on and who was just giving me lip service.

I spent the next few days unpacking, hanging pictures, and filling up my china cabinet with all of my treasures. I made a list of the things I decided I could live without and decided I would ask my children if they wanted anything I was willing to part with before I called the Salvation Army to come get it.

When I called them, they made it very clear that they had no use for Aunt Ginny's china or Grandma Miller's depression glass. My children said that they also needed to downsize and get organized with all their own items so they certainly didn't want to take on more "stuff" they would never use. So much for handing things down to my children. I was hurt that many of the items I was offering had been used through their childhood but still meant nothing to them. I guessed when I was gone they would just come in here, box up everything and either take it to the dump or give it to charity. Knowing that, I went over in my mind again what I really wanted to keep and what I would give away. I decided I could sell many of the antiques I still had but couldn't store, and use the money for something I wanted.

I avoided the community room and only went to the mailbox when I thought the crowd had dissipated. I did run into a few others in the hallway or in the parking lot, and they were very friendly so I started to believe that the run-in I had experienced with Marianne was a fluke, and I should give the others here the benefit of the doubt. So, after I packed up my entire car with boxes and bags of unwanted items and dropped them off at a thrift store, I went to the community room again and had a very good time sharing stories with some of the other residents, It was a much more pleasant time than the previous encounter.

Chapter 7
The Laundry

One day I decided to check out the laundry facility, so I loaded my whites and darks into my laundry basket, grabbed my roll of quarters and laundry detergent, and headed down the hall to the laundry room. When I arrived, I noticed both washing machines were occupied, so I returned to my apartment and set the timer on my microwave for 30 minutes. That way I wouldn't forget to check the washers again. When the timer went off, I headed down the hall. Now both dryers were occupied and both washers were also being used. Maybe I should check the laundry rooms on the other floors. Alas, every machine was being used. Maybe I should just wait until another day because Tuesday was obviously the day everyone did their laundry.

On Wednesday, I tried again. I was getting desperate because my clean underwear was dwindling. I could wash out my underwear in the bathroom sink but I didn't want to go out and buy more clothes when all I needed was an available washing machine and dryer.

I headed down the hall to the laundry room, and before I even arrived, I could hear the washers swishing away which meant that I had missed my chance again. Yup, both washers and dryers were operating at full speed. I didn't want a repeat of yesterday, so I headed down to the 2nd floor right away to see if I could catch a break and find an available machine. Not a chance. All four machines were working overtime washing and drying other people's underwear.

This same scenario repeated itself every hour until about 11:00 pm when I was too tired to start my laundry. I wondered how many clothes these people owned. Finally, on Thursday at 6:00 am I found both washers and dryers open on my floor. After loading my clothes, detergent, and quarters into the machine, I gave a sigh of relief.

While waiting for the washers to do their job I decided to get a cup of coffee in the community room where I found Tootsie. I joined her and relayed what I had been experiencing with the laundry. At this point I had to laugh at the absurdity of the situation and chalked it up to being new in the building and not being familiar with "the rules."

Tootsie looked at me in alarm and said, "You didn't use the machines on your floor just now did you?" When I stated that I had indeed taken advantage of the unoccupied machines Tootsie groaned. "Oh no, Betty, you can't use that laundry on Thursdays. Didn't anyone tell you that when you moved in?" I replied, "The only thing I was told was that the laundry rooms are for everyone's use from 6:00 am - 10:00 pm every day."

Tootsie just stared at me in disbelief. "I am afraid you might have stepped on someone's toes by using the laundry right now."

"Whose toes would that be?" I asked.

"Marianne's," said Tootsie.

I broke out in a sweat. If there was one person I did not want to piss off, it was Marianne, the parking guru.

"I am sure it will be fine. I'll be finished with my laundry by about 7:30, so she will have all day to use the machines," I said.

"Oh no, you don't understand, Betty. There are certain people here that sort of run the place, or think they do, and you do not want to get on their bad side," said Tootsie.

"Well, my clothes are already in the washers, so I can't do anything about it now. I will just get out of the laundry room as fast as possible and be more careful next time," I said, almost believing my own hype.

Tootsie suggested that we go up and check on my laundry. Maybe they would be ready to put in the dryer, and I could avoid any unpleasantness with Marianne. When we arrived, we discovered that my clothes had been removed, wringing wet, from the washers and deposited in the laundry tub. The washers were humming along blissfully with someone else's clothes in them. "Oh dear, we are too late," moaned Tootsie.

I was amazed at some people's determination to get their way. My heart was heavy, and I felt like I had been run over by a steamroller. Now what was I going to do? I decided that two could play at this game and asked Tootsie to help me take the clothes out of the washers and put mine back in. We would replace my clothes with theirs in the laundry tub. I would then sit there protecting my laundry until it was done and ready for the dryer.

"Oh, my God, no," shrieked Tootsie. "I don't think that is a good idea. You don't want her to know it was you who moved her clothes. If she finds you here, she will be really angry and find some way to retaliate."

I told Tootsie I was not going to give into a bully at this stage of my life and that Marianne would have to deal with me face to face. I told her she did not have to wait with me if it made her uncomfortable. She started to tremble, turned the color of ash, and flew out of the room.

All of a sudden, a shadow fell across the room. Marianne filled up the entire doorway with her buxom body, legs splayed, hands on her hips with a look on her face that could freeze a hot tamale.

With her flaming red hair (dyed, of course) and wild eyebrows that hadn't see a tweezers in many months, I could understand why she frightened people. "What is going on in here?" she bellowed.

"I am doing my laundry," I stated sweetly as I smiled at her and turned another page in a two- year - old *Popular Gardens* magazine.

"Where did you put my clothes?" she snarled.

"I put them in the same place that you put mine. In the laundry tub," still speaking calmly I explained. "I knew you wouldn't mind because I was here first, and it states in our resident handbook that there is no way to reserve a spot in the laundry facilities, same as with the parking."

I thought Marianne would attack me, but she just turned abruptly and walked out the door. "Whew," I said to myself. I dodged a bullet this time. I proceeded to finish my laundry and returned to my apartment. Shortly after, Tootsie was knocking at my door.

"Oh, I am so glad to see you are all right. I saw Marianne walking towards the laundry room. I was worried she would do something rash, and then you would decide to move out."

"No, I am fine. People like her need to learn to respect others and get along. I can't believe she has any friends here."

"Well, I wouldn't call them friends," Tootsie said. "Everyone is just frightened of her because she is so bossy and downright scary looking. If she doesn't get her own way, she can get really mean and verbally abusive."

"Why do people put up with her?" I asked. "Why don't they just ignore her or stand up to her?"

"I really don't know," Tootsie puzzled. "It has been like this ever since I moved in. I think that because some people have been here since the building was new, they feel like they own the place. Some of the managers have not helped the situation because they have given into her and her group for years. It is easier for Linda to just give in than to fight for the rest of us. Although, Linda has stood up to Marianne a few times when she first started working here and some things have changed because of that, but in the big picture, most of us will not take her on because we never know what she will do." "One time," Tootsie continued. "When someone new parked in one of the spots that Marianne thinks are unavailable to the rest of us, she drew her car up right behind them and waited for them to come out of the building. When Nancy came out, she asked what was going on. Marianne told her this is what happens when you park in the wrong place. Nancy calmly pulled out her cell phone and called 911. When the police arrived, Marianne was livid because they gave her a ticket for obstructing traffic. Oh Boy! You should have heard the horrible names that Marianne called Nancy. Naturally, Marianne had to move her car, and Nancy just left hers where she was parked until the next day. Ever since then, Marianne has had it in for Nancy and tried to make her life miserable. But Nancy just played it cool and ignored Marianne, which only made her angrier. You would think that some people here were back in Junior High school."

I thought back to when Larry was still alive. When I was married, we both had our own opinions and ideas, but we cooperated so that we both came out feeling like we had won. Isn't that what adults do? I made up my mind I would treat everyone with the same dignity and respect they showed me. Little did I know the promise I just made was not going to come to fruition.

Chapter 8
The First Writing Group

I was told there was a good library in the building and there was also a writing group I could join. It would give me the opportunity to meet some other people. There was also an occasional potluck dinner, a bingo game every week, and a card club. It sounded like I could be as busy as I wanted to be. I decided to check out the writing group the next week.

What they didn't tell me about the writing group was there was a "leader," named Stella Watson, and she decided what topic we would write about every two weeks. So, this wasn't the "creative writing" class I had hoped for, but I gave it a try anyway.

Stella choose topics for the group like, "What was your favorite vacation? Who was your favorite teacher? When was the first time you were on an airplane?" All these were great topics if we were sitting around having lunch, but this was supposed to be a creative writing class where we could express our ideas and make up stories that would entertain the readers.

I was involved for about a month when I made a suggestion that it might be more creative if we chose our own topics. That way we could write about anything we wanted to and share it with the group. The room became silent. Everyone looked at the Stella. I thought, "Oh no, what would she say about this?"

Stella calmly stated that if the group dynamics were going to change, she would probably need to drop out. Silence, dead silence.

Finally, I worked up enough nerve to say, "Why would you have to do that?"

Stella said, "This is just how I have always run this group, and I don't like change."

It turned out that Stella was one of the original occupants at Eden Estates and had lived here twenty years. I said, "No, please don't quit. This has been your group all these years, and I am a newcomer here."

"Are you sure about that?" Stella asked tearfully.

"Yes, I am sure."

As I went back to my apartment, I already decided this group was not for me and I wouldn't be returning. If the others were happy with the way Stella ran the group, then God bless them. I would find other ways to use my creativity. I knew that some of the local school districts offered classes on many different subjects, and I would definitely be looking into those.

In fact, now that I was reminded of this, I needed to give some thought to the people in other parts of my life, like my writing group, as suspects for my murder. I couldn't eliminate anyone just yet. Everyone I knew were suspects — friends, neighbors, acquaintances, everybody. I was feeling like I couldn't trust anyone.

Chapter 9
The Second Writing Group

I had found a community creative writing class at a high school about five miles from my apartment, and they were just about to start a new session. I signed up just in time and looked forward to beginning a new challenge.

I was excited the next Monday when I left for my first writing class. I had never attended a class like this where I didn't know anyone and had no idea of what to expect. I assumed we would be writing something each week and then reading it to the class the next week. I was a little apprehensive about reading my little stories, but I also wanted to learn how to write more creatively. I thought of this as just another adventure I was going to undertake to make my new lifestyle happier and more interesting.

Tony Thomas was the creative writing instructor. He was a former composition and literature teacher at this very school, but had retired the year before. He said he was bored just sitting home, so he approached the school about teaching this class to budding, new authors. The school jumped at the chance because he had been one of the favorite teachers in the school, and because he had taught for 30 years, he certainly knew his craft. Plus, both the school and Mr. Thomas could make a little money from the class.

That Monday there were five other people in the class when I arrived in room 318 at Abraham Lincoln High School. There were some young people, some old people, some seasoned, and some beginners. I liked that there was a cross section of people involved, both male and female.

After Mr. Thomas gave us a short synopsis of the course and told us about his experience, and he asked that we call him Tony and looked to us to introduce ourselves.

The first person who spoke was Mandy, a wife and mother of three, who had always wanted to write stories but didn't know how to get started. "My kids take up most of my time, but after I have put them all to bed and with my husband working nights, I like to curl up in front of the fireplace with my computer and just let my mind flow. I have started writing many stories, but I always get caught up in not knowing if I am using the correct grammar or syntax, and I would like to learn how to make my writing interesting and easy to read." Mandy had a beautiful smile and I felt she was sincere about learning along with the rest of us.

Next, there was a retired gentleman who liked writing fantasy stories. He would make up entire civilizations with funny and wonderful adventures. Jerry had already had some of his prose published in a few magazines, but he was having trouble knowing how to move forward. "I just get stuck looking at my pad of paper and my mind goes blank. I hope I can learn how to get over that." He was also concerned if what he was writing would be appealing to a larger audience. "I don't want to bore people to tears when they read my stories. When I was younger, I would go to some of the coffee houses in Brooklyn and read on open mic night. We were all what you would call flower children back then so I don't know if the audience really liked my readings or if they were all so stoned they just clapped at anything anyone read. I want to get more serious with my writing now and can use all the help I can get. I am very open to criticism if that will make me a better writer."

We moved on to a very nice looking man about my own age. Cory shared, "After my wife died a few years ago, I was very lonely. My therapist advised me to write down my thoughts and feelings about my wife and our life together. She said that if I concentrated on all the wonderful years we had together, it might put my grief in a whole new light. So, I started writing every single day. As I wrote and the memories came flooding back, I discovered that I was grieving the life I wish we had, not the one we actually lived. I let my therapist read some of what I wrote, and she was very complementary suggesting I take a creative writing class. So here I am." Cory seemed like a very nice man, and I thought I would enjoy being in class with him. I found it refreshing that a man my age was willing to write about his feelings.

We moved on to Ellen who simply said, "I like to write stories about my life, but I don't know if they are any good. I came here primarily to get help with composition, but also content. I think I have led a very interesting life, but I would like to put it down on paper in a manner that other people would enjoy reading. The way I am proceeding now, it sounds very factual but boring. I want to learn how to use dialog so the stories are more enjoyable and easier to understand."

We all nodded our heads like we had been experiencing the same problems in our writing. It was beginning to look like a very compatible group. I decided my apprehension was all in my head, and I would learn a lot from everyone here.

I then introduced myself and said I loved to write short stories, both fiction and nonfiction but I also needed help putting my thoughts down on paper in a cohesive manner. I said, "I have all these wonderful ideas swimming around in my head, and I lay awake at nights practicing how I will form the sentences and paragraphs. However, when I wake up the next morning, it has all been erased from my mind, and I have to start from scratch. When I finally sit in front of my computer, I don't know where to start. The thoughts are in my head, but they just won't go down my fingers to the keyboard." Several people nodded again.

Then there was Norman. He went on and on about how many articles and books he already had published. Everything from stories in *Reader's Digest* to a novel about the northwest part of Washington near the Canadian border. The rest of us looked at each other as if to say, "What is he doing in this class?"

Norman said, "I suppose I don't really need this class, but I am getting into a little rut and am having trouble getting started again. I thought if I joined a class where I was required to write something every week, I would get over my slump. Also, with my experience, I could probably be very helpful to the rest of you."

Tony just shook his head probably thinking, "Great, all I need is someone who thinks they know more than I do and will be sharing with all these beginners his pearls of wisdom."

Margarette was last. I would put her age at about fifty. She also had been seeing a therapist who had told her writing about her past was an excellent way to deal with emotions she couldn't let go of. She said she had been writing a lot, and because she was forced to relive some very painful memories, she had actually been able to work through some of her pain and move on to other feelings and memories that were still troubling her. Margarette said she used a lot of humor in her writings to mask the hard truth and found it easier to deal with feelings when the facts were put forward in a more light-hearted manner. She was also starting to write funny stories about her children and current family life. I thought Margarette was very brave to have even shown up here with complete strangers when she didn't know how they would respond to her very personal writings.

I remember thinking this was going to be more interesting than I first expected. I knew I was going to look forward to Mondays from now on. After listening to all the students that I was going to spend many nights with, I felt much better about my decision to join the class. I had a feeling we were going to learn a lot from each other in the next few months. I went home happy.

The next Monday was very interesting. Not everyone had written something for the class, or at least they were not willing to share it. Tony asked for volunteers to read their stories.

Cory wanted to go first. He had written a story about a time during the Vietnam War when he was an Army Sergeant with 30 men under his command. He was only 25 years old but carried so much responsibility that he went through most days high from smoking pot. It was the only way that he and his men could continue to raid villages and burn them to the ground leaving innocent people with nothing. They would also take whatever they wanted, including the virginity of many young women, and not feel at all guilty. He knew in his heart this was not who he was, but he had to prove to his men he was in command of the situation.

When he was drafted, he had just graduated from college and was looking forward to starting a career as a mechanical drafter. There were several positions he was interested in, but he never got the chance to use his hard-earned skills. He was very angry about being drafted and actually considered fleeing to Canada, but he felt his father, who had fought in Europe during WWII, would have disowned him.

While Cory was reading his story, I could tell his sharing this horrifying time with us was therapeutic for him. He didn't know any of us or how we felt about this time in our history, and the way he wrote was almost clinical, like he was reading a newspaper to us. I wondered about his motive for sharing these facts about his life with people he had just met. It must have been so traumatic that it was still, after all these years, haunting him. Cory said he believed what had happened to him in Viet Nam had a great bearing on his marriage. He had a very hard time expressing his true feelings, and that didn't bode well with his wife.

It was hard for me to imagine anything so painful, both physically and emotionally, that it would still have repercussions for me now. I would be interested in knowing where this story was going. Maybe next week.

We only had time for one more story, and Tony chose me to read next. I had written about my father and what a wonderful man he was. I told about us going fishing together and how that was really the only time I had alone with him. I missed him during the week when he worked nights on the railroad, so I treasured our time together on the weekends. Since my mother was a very controlling and abusive parent, I thought I would die if I didn't get to spend as much time with Dad as I could. He balanced her abuse with kindness and attention. I don't think he was ever aware how I was treated by my mother during the time he was at work, but even if he did, he would never confront her. In a way, my mother was a lot like Marianne. She was a large woman who got what she wanted by being an outrageous bully.

My dad was gentle and loving, and he never made me feel stupid or lazy. Dad praised me for being a creative person and always liked the pictures I painted. He was patient and kind and really the only reason I survived my childhood with some semblance of sanity.

The room was very quiet as I read my story. At the end, everyone told me they could tell how I felt about my dad and why. I was so happy to have gotten my point across in a cohesive manner. Some of the people in the class had obviously experienced many of the same feelings in their own childhoods. Sometimes it is the bad in our lives that connect us to one another, not the happy ones.

After class, some of the people wanted to go out for coffee at a nearby cafe, and they invited me along. I was happy to continue the discussions that had started in class, and since it was only 8:00 pm I was not looking forward to going home to my small, empty apartment.

After we had taken seats in the little café near the school, we scanned the menu. I am sure many of us were debating whether to just have coffee or pair it with one of the scrumptious desserts pictured. I decided that coffee was enough for me even though the apple pie ala mode looked divine.

After we had placed our orders, Norman shared, "I didn't have time to write anything this week. I was really busy and had no time for anything but work. I got a very large order for windows, and I had to spend a lot of time on the job site making sure my employees were doing everything correctly. You know those spics, they will lay down on the job every chance they get. I have to be on them every minute."

I did not want this moment to pass by without confronting Norman. So, I said. "Norman, are the people you employ here legally or are you paying them cheap wages under the table?"

"I can't afford to pay legal immigrants or white people. They want high wages, worker's comp insurance, and a 401k plan. I wouldn't make any money if I hired them, so I hire anyone who is available and will work for less money. I pay them in cash. This is just the way business is done today, if you are smart."

I was so happy when Jerry spoke up and said, "I owned my own HVAC business for many years, and I made sure every one of my workers was paid a fair wage and were covered by insurance in case something happened to them on the job. I had workers from every ethnic background, and I made sure they all had a green card if it was necessary. I checked their backgrounds before I hired them so when I was taking care of them, I knew they would be fair to me and my company as well. We were all in it together, and when we were very busy, I would be working right beside them to get the work done on time. I trusted them to work on my house or my family's houses, which they did many times. I made a very good living, and so did my employees." Jerry spoke very forcefully in order to get his point across to Norman.

The rest of us looked at each other and felt very uncomfortable, but were glad that Jerry spoke up. I am sure we were all grateful we didn't work for Norman's company.

Shortly, we all said we needed to get going, so the group broke up and went our own ways. I stopped Jerry and told him how proud I was when he spoke up to Norman.

"Guys like that just bug me," Jerry said. "Always cutting corners to make a buck. I wouldn't buy windows from him if he was the cheapest bid I got. Norm doesn't realize that if one of his workers gets hurt on the job, they can sue him, and he could lose everything he is trying so hard to hang onto. I didn't run my business the way I did just because I am a nice guy, it was also because it was smart and the right thing to do. I am glad you agree with me. See you next week, Betty."

I couldn't wait for Monday.

We continued meeting in our writing class for several months, getting to know each other on many levels through our stories, and visiting after the class. I thought it funny that Norman never missed a class but always had a good reason why he didn't have anything but advice for the rest of us. He was too busy to contribute anything and a lot of us started to think he was really only a want-to-be- author, not truly an already published one.

Mandy wrote delightful stories about her children and all the foibles that occurred in their everyday lives. Tony told her he was sure she would be able publish her stories because she had a very entertaining way of making children's ordinary antics and problems sound amusing. Most of us couldn't wait for the next chapter.

As the weeks went on, Cory continued writing about his experiences during the Vietnam War, but they became more about his feelings and less about what he and his men had experienced. He said it really helped putting these emotions down on paper and sharing them with people he knew wouldn't judge him for actions he took all those years ago. He had been a young man, following orders, and learning some of life's hardest lessons that he would carry with him his entire life. Cory actually started writing about other parts of his life in a much lighter manner, and we found out he could be very funny and caring. He said it was a side of himself he was not sure would ever return after his earlier experiences. All of us could see him blossoming in his writing and were happy to be a part of his emerging new personality.

I wrote about many subjects and was feeling more comfortable sharing my stories and things about my personal life during the time we spent in the little café after class. We talked about our families, careers, ex-husbands and wives, and how much we enjoyed the writing class. We were really starting to gel as a group, and Monday nights became my favorite time of the week.

Both Ellen and Marguerite had come a long way in their writing, and I could tell they were feeling much more comfortable sharing their most private inner thoughts with the group, except with Norman who always had advice for them when they were done reading. Not about their writing, but about their personal lives. I remember distinctly when I had finally had enough of his meddling. I said, "Norman, where did you get your license to practice psychology? I thought you sold windows, or is this just a second job for you? Have been holding out on us? I don't think anyone comes here to get advice about their lives because I have never heard anyone ask you for it. Now, if you have something to say about what was read tonight, feel free to make comments about it, but if you are going to just give unsolicited advice once again, I think everyone here would prefer you keep it to yourself." I thought I heard several snickers going through the group and Ellen mouthed a silent, "Thank you" in my direction.

Tony said he had to go home and he would see us all the next week. As he was leaving, he made a point to tell Norman he expected him to have something to read next week. If he couldn't think of anything to write about, maybe this class wasn't really what he had been looking for. Tony said, "Norman, I know you have written many stories, so if you can't come up with a new tale, just read something that you wrote earlier. I think the point is to hear something from everyone each week. It just isn't fair to the other people if you don't contribute."

The rest of us silently hoped Norman would take the hint and just stop coming. He added nothing to the class but tension and embarrassment. The rest of us took this class seriously. We worked hard and took the positive criticism to heart in order to better our writing skills. I felt Norman was afraid to read anything he wrote because he was afraid of the feedback he would get. That told me he didn't have much confidence in his ability to put something cohesive down on paper. It was sad, really.

Chapter 10
The Potluck

One Monday there was a notice posted on the bulletin board by the mailboxes that there was going to be a potluck dinner in the community room on the following Friday at 4:00. I guessed it was true that some older people liked to eat dinner early. There was a sign-up sheet with a few names on it so, I added mine noting I would bring a veggie tray that included three different dips. I thought that would be a healthy choice for us seniors and easy for me to pick up at the deli across the street.

When Friday arrived, I started getting my food together about 3:45. As I left the elevator on the first floor, I heard what sounded like a large crowd of people in the community room. As I entered, there were more people gathered in that one spot than I had ever seen here before. I put my contribution on the serving table and noticed that most of the food was already gone, and it was just 3:55. All the tables were occupied, some with extra chairs pulled up to them to allow more people to eat there. Most of the plates were empty and piled in the center of each table. I felt like a guest who had come late to the party.

It did seem there were an inordinate amount of sweets on the buffet table compared to the rest of the fare. There had been some salads on the table but mostly chips and dip, cream cheese puffs, and cocktail wieners in barbecue sauce along with pies, cakes and cookies filling out the menu. I had obviously been mistaken when I thought there would be several salads and other healthy options.

As I looked around, Tootsie called my name and asked if I wanted to join her and the others at her table. I signaled that I would join them in a few minutes after I found a plate and filled it with acceptable fare. What I ended up with was a lot of the veggies I had brought and a couple of chips.

Joining Tootsie at her table, she introduced the others at the table. "Betty, this is Carolyn Casey, Audrey Swanson, Shirley Duxbury, and of course you have already met JoAnn. Everyone, this is Betty Nelson. She just moved in a few weeks ago, and she has already been attacked by Marianne."

"Oh no", said Carolyn. "It usually takes her a lot longer to skewer a new resident. You must have set a new record. Congratulations, Betty." The rest of the ladies laughed and told me I was welcome to join them anytime. It became very clear, after spending time with these women, I would probably become friends with them. It felt good to know there were several people I could count on or ask for help. It was also very clear that Marianne, Carol and Audrey would never be people I could be friends with or even trust.

There were only three people sitting at Marianne's table, and they kept glancing over at us and whispering among themselves. We ignored Marianne and her sidekicks and spent a couple of hours getting acquainted. We laughed and had a great time sharing stories about our lives and how we ended up at Eden Estates.

When the evening was coming to the end (at 6:00pm), most of the people grabbed the dishes they had brought to the meal and walked out of the room leaving plates piled everywhere and the tables a mess. Tootsie and the others at our table started clearing off the tables and loading the dishwasher. I joined in the effort by taking out the garbage, wiping down the tables and vacuuming the carpet. We rearranged the community room to its original configuration. When we were finished, everything was as it should be to start the next day, and we turned out the lights and went home feeling contented.

I didn't realize at the time this process was going to repeat itself every time there was food in the community room. I thought to myself, "Didn't these people keep house for several years before moving here? Is this the way they kept their kitchens back when they were raising their families?" I decided the reason some people were so inconsiderate was because they knew there were people like me, Tootsie, Audrey and JoAnne who would clean up after them because we didn't like a dirty community room or kitchen. We talked about not cleaning up after everyone else, but none of us wanted to live in a dirty building just to spite people we didn't even like.

Chapter 11
Bowling

    I continued to think about different times in the past that would raise someone's ire with me enough to do me in and the time we went bowling might be a possibility.

    The management asked that we sign up to go for an afternoon of bowling because they thought it might bring us closer together. Oh brother, was Linda wrong about that. Naturally, the team leaders (Marianne and myself) wanted to have their friends on their team but Linda put together teams consisting of some people we got along with and some we didn't. She was hoping if we got to know each other at an event that didn't involve being at Eden Estates, we may find some common ground to enable all of us to see commonalities among ourselves instead of just the differences.

    Marianne was paired with Tootsie, JoAnn, and Maureen. Besides myself, my team consisted of Carol, Nancy, and Elaine. There were four teams all together, so we took an activity bus to the bowling alley. Residents who were not able to participate in the bowling came along to cheer for their favorite teams.

    While I was choosing a ball, Maureen came right behind me and grabbed every ball I had rejected for being too heavy, too light, or that my fingers got stuck in. When I finally found one I thought would work, Maureen tried to grab it out of my hands declaring she had spotted it first. There we were, in the middle of the bowling alley, with both of us holding onto a ball like our lives depended on it. I finally gave in and let go of the ball. At the same time, Maureen was tugging with all her might in order to get the ball out of my hands. She went reeling backwards with a ten-pound ball clutched in her hands adding to the force she was experiencing until she came to an abrupt halt as she landed half way down the alley flat on her fanny. When Maureen went down with a grunt on her gluteus maximus, it drew the attention of several other bowlers, and they all started laughing.

    One man in the next alley said, "Didn't anyone tell her she was supposed to let go of the ball when she threw it down the alley?"

Maureen was more mortified than injured, but she made a big production of getting to her feet and limping back to a chair. Linda asked her if she was all right to bowl or if she wanted to sit out the game and Linda would take her place. Maureen squeaked that she was fine, but she limped over to her chair still holding the coveted ball. I had gone to choose a different ball that I felt was even better than the one Maureen held.

"Let the games begin," I thought.

I was reluctant to be the first one to start the game, but someone from Maureen's team wanted to make sure I was the first one to be humiliated. So, I was listed in position one on the scoreboard. Nowadays, unlike when I was a girl, the scoring was done automatically, so at least I didn't have to worry about Marianne cheating me out of any pins I knocked down.

The first ball I threw sent eight pins flying, and I was elated. After so many years away from the bowling alley, I felt for sure I would be throwing gutter ball after gutter ball. The next ball was not as accurate and did go into the gutter, but I still felt vindicated that I had knocked down any pins on the first try. Next, Marianne got up to bowl, and her foot slid over the foul line and her ball went into the gutter. A loud buzzer went off, and she turned a beautiful shade of purple. She was so flustered, she threw a gutter ball on her second shot also, so her score was zero for the first frame to my eight. I couldn't have been happier.

I had no idea Carol bowled on a senior league and was a very good bowler. I was wondering if she would intentionally bowl badly because she was on my team so her friend, Marianne, would win the day. However, Carol's ego would not let her throw the game, so when she got three strikes in a row, I thought Marianne would pop a blood vessel. She kept giving Carol dirty looks and made some inappropriate comments, but Carol ignored Marianne. I believe she did this because when we were all in the apartment building, Marianne always called the shots and embarrassed all of her friends. This was an opportunity for Carol to thumb her nose at Marianne. Because we were in a public place, Marianne couldn't do anything about it. Score one for my team!

Our teams took turns aiming for the pins at the end of the long alley, and when we finished two games, we were all exhausted. Some of the people who had participated in the event had done nothing more strenuous in the past several years than walking down the stairs to the community room from the second floor. Marianne had not been happy when she couldn't have her friends on her team, but now that my team had won the day and her friend Carol had been instrumental in our win, she was almost inconsolable. She accused us of cheating although we had several witnesses to the fact that we did nothing to interfere with their lackluster performance. Having Carol on my team was just too much for Marianne to swallow.

    I did not bowl as well as I wanted to, but beating Marianne's team was enough to give me some ideas about other contests we could participate in. Miniature golf came to mind. Also, bumper cars. Well, maybe not that, but if I could keep a competition going between me and Marianne, and of course beating her at every turn, maybe she would get off my case and just leave me alone. Every time I thought about the numerous episodes where Marianne and I had crossed swords, I became more and more convinced that it had to be her who took my life — maybe even with help from her cohorts. But, that sounded way too obvious.

Chapter 12
Shopping Trip

As the months went on, I learned the best times to go to the bank, the grocery store, and the thrift shop. Normally, I went with Tootsie or JoAnne, but today I was alone as I ran my errands. I waited months for the shoes I coveted to go on sale, and today was the day. I was pleased I was able to shop at several stores and not go over my budget. I loved coupons. When I returned to what I referred to as "the home", JoAnne met me at the door and convinced me to have a cup of coffee. As we sat down at a table, it was like someone had announced I was giving away hundred-dollar bills. Suddenly, our table was full and several other tables nearby were being taken over by busybodies. They started going through my shopping bags and making comments about everything I bought.

"Oh, let me see the shoes you just got," said Audrey. "Did you get them at DSW? How much were they? I saw some very similar ones at Wal-Mart a couple of weeks ago." After she had examined them closely she said, "Oh, I guess these may not be the same shoes I was thinking of. Those were a different color, the heals were higher, and they had a strap. Other than that, they are just the same."

JoAnne pulled my new bras out of another bag and was stretching the straps to see how comfortable they might be. "Why did you get them all the same color, and why did you choose nude?" I explained I liked the nude color so I could wear them under any top and they wouldn't show through.

Some of the food items I bought were opened and passed around the table. When I was putting my grocery bags into a cart so that I could take my purchases up to my apartment, I noticed the bananas were all gone, the cashews were absent from the jar of mixed nuts, and there were only about a dozen raspberries left in the carton. And these were my friends!

All of a sudden, I felt the need to explain everything I had purchased. They were going through my shopping bags like they were at a rummage sale, making disparaging remarks about every item they disliked, and asking how much I had paid for everything.

The ladies at the other tables were watching and listening like we were on a reality TV show and we were there for their entertainment. Some would say "be quiet" when they couldn't hear what the women at my table were saying. I felt my privacy had been invaded, and I didn't wasn't sure how to stop this circus.

I started grabbing my purchases, cramming them back into the bags and pushing the cart out of the room. As I left, people just stared at me like they could not believe my rudeness. I had learned my lesson. I was not going into the community room after I had just gone shopping.

Chapter 13
The Walking Club

Some of the women and I started a walking club. We would meet in the lobby every morning at 7:00 am to go for a walk, making use of the many trails available to us around the area. It was not only healthy but allowed us to talk about some of the more interesting people who lived at Eden Estates. Because we were laughing and talking, I am sure we walked a lot farther than we would have if we were on our own. The only problem was some of the women wanted to go one way and others wanted to take a different route. I didn't understand why anyone needed to fight about where to walk. I suggested, "Why doesn't everyone just walk where they want to and let the others either join them or go their own way?"

"I think that is a good idea," said Maureen. "I'd like to go down near the lake. Does anyone want to join me?" Several of us decided it would be fun to go to the lake and watch the ducks and geese. The trail was a little more challenging than the flat surface of the other trail, but we were doing this for exercise so we didn't mind.

When we arrived at the lake, there were several row boats with fishermen hoping to catch the big one. Most of them were retired gentlemen spending time with their buddies or grandchildren. We walked along the shore and cheered when one man fought with a fish he had just hooked. When he pulled his prize catch out of the water, it was a very large Northern Pike. The man held it up in the net to show all of us, and we were very happy for him. He then gently put the fish over the side of the boat, and it slipped back into the water. One of the man's friends had taken a picture of him with the fish so he could share this great experience with his family and friends at home.

At times like this, I believed life was good. I would carry this good feeling all the way home, and if I didn't run into one of the grumpy people, maybe the feeling would last all day.

We continued to walk most days that spring and not only did I lose weight, but I was able to make some wonderful connections with some of the people in the building that I had only a passing acquaintance with previously. When it rained, we would often go to the mall to do our walking. That gave us many opportunities to see interesting things with many subjects to talk about. We started playing a game where we would take turns picking out outfits for each other when we passed clothing stores. Tootsie always choose some ridiculous, skimpy outfit for me with thigh-high boots, leather vests, and very short skirts. If I could find an itsy-bitsy bikini in one of the store windows, I would automatically want to assign it to Tootsie. I was happy I was able to be involved with many different activities since I moved here.

Chapter 14
B-I-N-G-O

I remembered the many times I spent Wednesday evenings in the community room playing bingo, and I chuckled to myself. When I first started joining 12 to15 other residents for the weekly bingo games, we enjoyed the talent of another resident who had volunteered her services to call the game. Rosemary was a very good caller because she spoke clearly and loud enough for most people to hear the numbers. She also had a great sense of humor, and we spent a lot of the time laughing and having a good time.

Naturally, just like everything else that happen here, there were some problems created by just a few people. One thing that never changed was where everyone sat. Not only was it important that they sat at the same table with the same people, but they had to sit in the same chair each week. When I went down for my first attempt at playing bingo, I had no idea about these unspoken rules.

As I entered the room, I looked around for any familiar faces. Luckily, Tootsie and JoAnn were sitting at a table and flagged me over to sit with them. Neither of my friends cared where they sat, so they offered me a chair at their table. Then they took me over to the table where I could choose the bingo cards I would use that night. I had no trouble picking cards because I believed this was a game of chance so the cards didn't matter. Two women who had just entered the room came rushing over to the table where the bingo cards were displayed. They started pawing their way through the cards left and, for some reason, were getting more and more upset the more they looked. They started looking around at me like I had just kidnapped their first-born child. I sat down and started getting ready to play the game when Amelia came over to our table and said to me, "Betty, I want to see the cards you chose."

"Why would you want to do that?"

"I want to make sure you didn't take my cards." Oh no, I thought to myself. Is this going to be another situation like the parking problem or using the laundry rooms?

Tootsie responded, "Amelia, leave Betty alone. This is Betty's first time playing bingo here, and she just took the first three cards on the top of the pile."

"Well, how do you know whether she took my special cards? I do really well with those cards, and I marked them so I could tell them apart from the others."

I looked at Amelia and handed her the cards I had chosen. Evidently, I had not taken her cards, and she threw them back at me and turned to look at everyone else in the room. She knew if her cards were not in the pile or in my hands, somebody else had her cards. Nobody looked at her as she scanned the room for the guilty party, nor did they offer to let her peruse their cards.

Amelia went back to the table and chose a couple of cards plunking her large bottom down in a chair at the only empty table in the room. Her friend, Clara, looked embarrassed but joined Amelia at her table where she sat in the "wrong chair" and was told by Amelia to immediately move to another one.

I was beginning to have second thoughts about this bingo activity. If there had been this much drama just getting ready for the game, I couldn't wait to see what happened when the game began.

Each week bingo was played, we paid a dime for each card. Most of the players played only one card at a time, but feeling daring, I chose three.

Susie was in charge of collecting the money before each game. There was a small bowl at each table where the players put in their dimes. After Susie collected the money, Rosemary said in a clear voice, "Time to play bingo. Game one." Everyone calmed down and looked expectantly at Rosemary.

"B-9," said Rosemary. There were a couple of "Yikes". I guessed some people had B-9 on their cards. Rosemary continued, "I-18, O-75, B-12, G-48." On and on it went.

One woman obviously had a hearing problem because every couple of numbers that were called, she spoke up in a high, squeaky voice, "Did you say B-6 or B-7?" Rosemary would repeat the number, and the game went on. Some people became upset that the game kept being interrupted and grumbled among themselves, but the game continued.

There was another distraction that started out at one table and grew to include several others. Every time a number was called, someone would say out loud something like, "Oh, I have I-25, not 24, just my luck." Or "I only need O-70, and I will have a bingo." The noise got louder and louder even though Rosemary warned these people that if the noise continued she would not be calling the game anymore. Every time those people started up again, someone in the room would say, "SHHHHHH." That usually worked, but whoever was brave enough to tell them to be quiet received a dirty look from someone at that table. I felt like I was in junior-high again.

Helen had a hard time seeing her numbers, and one of the others at her table would watch both her own cards and Helen's. Every few minutes you could hear Nancy whisper to Helen, "You have a B-3 on your card. Cover it with a chip." No one minded this happening because, after all, Nancy was being kind to Helen and most of us understood that someday we could all be in the same situation where we needed help playing bingo.

When G-57 was called, I looked down. I had a Bingo on one of my cards. "Bingo," I shouted.

I heard several people say, "On no, I only needed one more number."

Rosemary asked me to call back the numbers that I had on my card. "B-12, I-18, N-43, G-57, O-62".

"That's a good bingo," said Rosemary. Susie came over and gave me my winnings — $3.30. I remember thinking that this might be more fun than I had previously thought, but it was probably beginner's luck.

After the eighth game, we took a break for coffee and bars that one of the players brought to share. Even during the break, everyone still sat at the same tables where they were playing the game. I was disappointed there was not very much visiting during the break, but I had to remember there were unspoken rules surrounding this ritual.

As the evening went on, there were two people who won many more games than anyone else. Rebecca, who had not won even one game, exclaimed it had to be her bad luck cards and exchanged them for two different cards.

The sixteenth game was a cover-all. It took a lot longer, and the tension in the room was palpable. After all, the prize was double the normal pot which could mean $6 - $7 was at stake. Everyone wanted to win the cover-all, but only one person would win. Luckily for me, I won the last game. Not everyone was happy about it because, after all, I was new to the game and they had been playing for years. To them, it didn't seem fair that I had just started playing so had not contributed to their winnings over the years, but they decided not to voice their feelings while I was in the room.

When the game was over, a few of us started cleaning up the bingo paraphernalia: bingo cards, cups for the money, poker chips, and coffee cups.

The other dozen or so players just took their keys and left the room. Tootsie, myself, and two others finished cleaning up the room including the kitchen. We emptied the coffee pots and loaded up the dishwasher with all the cups and plates that had been used. After we washed the tables and pushed in all of the chairs, we turned out the lights and went to our respective apartments. There was a deja vu feeling about this process because I knew the same people had done this before (after the potluck, birthday parties, etc.).

Chapter 15
Charlie

I had lived at Eden Estates for about three months when I was again surprised by a tenant I had never seen before. Several of us were enjoying a cup of coffee, and I had my back to the doorway. All of a sudden, JoAnn, who was sitting across the table from me, looked startled and whispered to us, "Don't look up, don't look up, don't look up. 'You know who' at 12 o'clock."

Everyone at the table froze in place. They all became very busy checking their phones, looking out the window, or examining their finger nails.

Shortly, a man (one of ten who lived in the building) pulled a chair up to our table and looked right at me. He was a smarmy looking character with all of the accoutrements of a "stud muffin" from the 1970's, including gold chains hanging around his neck where his shirt was opened to expose masses of gray chest hair. The thinning hair on his head was slicked back with what I guessed to be Brylcreem, and his one gold front tooth was just frosting on the cake. It was all I could do to not laugh out loud.

"Leave her alone, Charlie!" said Audrey. "We are trying to convince her this is a fun and respectable place to live.

"Oh, good" Charlie sneered, staring at a body part just below my neck. "Just what I like, fresh meat. We could make beautiful music together, baby. Any time you want a little action, just stroll on up to apartment 408, and I will show you a good time like you have never had before."

I turned in my chair so I could look him right in the eyes and said, "I've heard all about you Charlie, and let me give you some advice. I don't take crap from anyone and especially not a twelve-year-old boy in a 70 year-old body. If you ever say anything like that to me, or any woman here again, I will contact my lawyer and file a sexual harassment suit against you. If I need to, I will also go to the police department and get a restraining order against you. Take this to heart, if you see me in the hallway, just turn around and walk the other way. Am I making myself clear, big boy?" Everyone in the room started to applaud and cheer.

Charlie rose from his chair and with an embarrassed grin said, "I was just trying to be friendly. If you can't take a joke, that's your problem." He made a big production of leaving the room at his own slow pace when I'll bet he wanted to run like a scared rabbit.

I had been concerned that all the men in this building were going to be like Charlie Burns, but my friends convinced me he was the only blatantly stupid one in the bunch. It was rare to see most of the male residents. I don't think they felt very comfortable in the common areas of the building because they were so outnumbered by the fifty women who lived there and seemed to be everywhere. So the men mostly kept to themselves.

I was told that some of the men still worked full time, and two were employed locally on a part time basis so I wouldn't see these men very often. It wasn't that they were antisocial, just that they were very busy.

There were also several women I seldom saw because they had many different volunteer opportunities or did daycare for their grandchildren. Unfortunately, there were also many people who never left the building. Some had physical limitations that required them to use walkers or wheelchairs limiting their ability to move around freely. Others just seemed content to work on a puzzle day after day or sit in the community room having coffee with anyone who entered. I will not make judgements about these people, but I found it strange that even those who were healthy enough to leave the building, seldom did. Many people only left when they had doctor's appointments or family commitments. I think everyone had to live the life that made them happy. The only residents who made my toes curl were the ones who complained about being bored but never thought about doing something for other people or taking up a hobby they could do even in their own apartments. I decided there were people in the world who enjoyed living with their misery.

Chapter 16
Cory

After several months, we started to form friendships in and out of the writing group. Ellen and I had lunch several times, and Cory and I enjoyed going to museums and galleries when there was an artist featured that we both enjoyed.

I wouldn't call what Cory and I did dating actually, but we spent a lot of time together. We laughed a lot, and I remember thinking I had more fun with Cory than I ever expected to ever have after my husband died.

We started going out to dinner almost every weekend and even spent a few weekends together at bed and breakfast establishments, in separate rooms of course, when we would drive up north to enjoy the fall weather and colorful landscape. I enjoyed taking photographs of the places we visited, and I would get 8 by 10 enlargements to put together a collage on my living room wall which I would change out seasonally. At one time, I had a darkroom in the basement of my house in Iowa, but I never thought I would be able really enjoy photography like that again.

After we returned from a weekend away, we were both feeling amorous, and I decided to invite Cory up for a drink. I didn't normally bring Cory up to my apartment because I didn't want the others in the building to know how much time Cory and I were spending together. It was none of their business, and it was not worth the harassment I would be subjected to.

We sent out for Egg Foo Young and watched a favorite movie on Netflix. It was getting late, but Cory was being more than a little romantic. I excused myself and changed into something more comfortable. I had been very nervous about taking the next step in this adult relationship, but I also felt it was time. When I returned to the living room Cory was nervous also but made it clear that he wanted to spend the night.

Cory obviously wanted this to happen because he was prepared. He went down the back stairs to retrieve his over-night bag and came up the same way to avoid detection. He was unaware that most of the people in this building went to bed by 10:00 pm, and it was already after midnight. I wondered how long this bag had been in his trunk and how long he had been hoping this would happen. I didn't dare ask him, however.

When we finally crawled into bed, Cory removed a small bottle from his shaving kit and showed it to me. It was a bottle of strawberry flavored massage oil. I read about how this oil was used in a situation like this, and I was kind of leery considering it had been a very long time since I had been this close to an unclothed man. I finally said, "What the heck, let's go for it."

We spread the oil on each other, and I have to say the lovemaking was very smooth and aromatic after that. It felt so good to have someone to share this with who I knew wouldn't judge what my body looked or felt like. If I thought the night was something to remember, when we woke up the next morning, it was a whole new situation. We had fallen asleep with the oil all over both of us, and we had become glued to the sheets during the night so could not move. We started laughing, but it hurt as the sticky sheets were pulling against our skin. Painful as it was, it also made us laugh even more. What a predicament we had created. After we quit giggling, we knew we had to come to some sort of decision about how to get out of bed without injuring ourselves further.

Cory suggested we roll ourselves up in the sheets and move to the side of the bed where we could hopefully stand up, sheets and all. We accomplished this task after many stops and starts, and there we stood, rolled up in two huge sheets next to the bed. Then we decided if we could make it to the shower, we could stand under the hot water and wait for the oil to get hot enough to become liquid again. Then we could pull the sheets off of us a little at a time. So, this is what we did, hopping to the bathroom because we couldn't walk and hoping not to fall over on the way. We finally arrived in the bathroom and learned a whole new meaning of the phrase, "Hopping into the shower."

We were standing under the shower spray and laughing like a couple of school kids. A vow was made that this was something we would never tell our children or grandchildren — or anyone else for that matter. It would be our little secret.

We got dressed, and because it was only 5:00 am, I told Cory it was probably a good idea if he left by the back door before the busy bodies woke up and started roaming the hallways. We shared a lingering goodbye and vowed to see each other again soon. I hoped this wasn't a situation that Cory got what he wanted from me so my phone would never ring again. I hoped I would hear his voice say, "Hello, beautiful." I could only wait and see.

I thought I had dodged a bullet until later in the morning I when I went down for my morning coffee, and there were several snickers when I entered the community room. Some came from my friends but most were started by Marianne and her group of lemmings.

"I saw a strange car in the back parking lot last night, and it was still there this morning," sneered Carol. "I wonder who the person was who drove that car and who they were visiting. I know we are not supposed to have overnight guests unless we tell the manager in advance in case there is a fire. Then they will know to look for non-residents in the ashes."

Tootsie spoke up, "Why do you think it is any of your business? I have had my granddaughter stay overnight when I had my cataract surgery, and I didn't tell the old manager. If everyone would keep their noses out of other's business, we will all be better off."

I stayed really quiet until Marianne looked right at me and said, "Well, I thought I saw a man with Betty coming into the building last night, and if I am not mistaken, he drove that little red job that doesn't belong here. I didn't see it leave until early this morning when I was out having a cigarette."

I couldn't abide by Marianne's attitude, so I blurted out. "Well, maybe I did have a guest last night, but we didn't do much sleeping." Even Marianne's jaw dropped.

Tootsie started laughing and said, "Good for you. Do you think Cory has any friends who would love to meet a cute, funny, available female?" We laughed about the situation as Marianne, Carol, and Maureen continued to gaze at us with their mouths hanging open. I had never seen that happen before.

Tootsie knew I had been seeing Cory, but up until now had no idea that we had taken our relationship to the new level the night before. But now that Tootsie did know what was going on, I knew I could trust her not to share the information. Because I couldn't keep my big mouth shut and not get sucked into Marianne's goading, the Mean Girls knew more than I wanted them to. I may have to rethink not telling Linda about my overnight guest. I knew that Marianne would be very happy to turn me in for breaking the rules, so if I could inform Linda first, it would really take the wind out of Marianne's sails when she went to Linda to tattle on me.

I started talking to Tootsie about our plans for the day. This put a stop to the tormenting Marianne wanted to use to embarrass me until I couldn't take it anymore, and she hoped I would reveal all that had happened the night before. I wouldn't give her the satisfaction.

Cory and I started spending most weekends together. It was nice sharing my interests with someone who enjoyed the same things. It wasn't even necessary for us to talk a lot when we were together. Sometimes we would go to a beautiful garden and just enjoy taking pictures and walking among the seasonal plantings. Cory was very knowledgeable about many subjects and was always willing to share information with me, and this included knowledge about gardens.

That fall we attended an arts festival in one of the towns just south of Margin. It was a beautiful drive on a sunny day, and we enjoyed the scenery along the route. The town of Briar was very small, and the arts festival was its biggest drawing point every year. People came from as far as 100 miles away to walk around this charming village enjoying the hospitality of the year-round residents. There was a small waterfall where many people sat at picnic tables to eat their lunch and take family photos with the waterfall acting as an especially beautiful backdrop.

I was impressed with the variety of arts and crafts on display. We saw wonderful nature photographs, stunning jewelry pieces, and wood carvings that I had a hard time believing had started out as a tree. We meandered up and down the aisles, enjoyed some fresh out of the oven scones with clotted cream and stopped to listen to a band playing music that would have been more at home during the 50's or 60's. It was a relief to not hear a punk rock band playing at 90 decibels.

In the late afternoon, we came upon a booth displaying beautiful stained glass. The artist had created a large variety of leaded glass projects —

everything from small Christmas ornaments to a very large window that would have been right at home in a church. Cory was looking at the prices and thought they were priced unreasonably high. He said, "How can she charge so much for a couple of pieces of glass that are just put together and soldered? I would give her only half of what she is asking."

I was stunned. I asked, "Have you ever worked with stained glass?"

"Of course not, but it doesn't look too hard."

"Well, Cory I have created several stained glass pieces, and I can tell you it is a lot more complicated and detail oriented than you would think. It is very time consuming when the artist starts by drawing their own patterns. It can take up to several months to create a window like that one over there in the corner. There are probably 100 pieces in that frame that had to be drawn, cut out with a glass cutter, shaped to size with a grinding wheel, wrapped in copper foil and then soldered into place. I would charge a lot more than she is asking for some of these pieces. When I was making stained glass projects, I paid $50 for a 12" x 18" plate of art glass, and that was just one color in a piece I did with10 different kinds of glass. I charged $2,500 for just the labor for that window, and the client paid up front for the glass, solder, and copper foil. She was thrilled with the results, and after I installed her window, several of her friends hired me to make lamps and windows for them also."

I was so keyed up, I was out of breath when I had finished my tirade, but I was very upset that Cory would make the comments he had without knowing the first thing about the skill it took to create beautiful glass projects.

"OK, so it is harder than I thought, but I still think she is asking too much for a lot of these pieces." I couldn't believe my ears. I asked Cory if we could step around the corner because I had something to say to him in private. I could tell he was reluctant to leave the security of the crowd, but he did follow me around a building away from the others.

"Cory, I have a question. Is there any subject on earth in which you are not an expert? It seems to me that no matter what we talk about, you know more about it than I do even if you have no experience with the subject matter. Can you ever be wrong? Do you ever make mistakes?"

Cory looked like I had tossed a glass of cold water in his face. He stammered, "Well of course I don't know everything, but I have done a lot of things in my life, and I read a lot of books about many different subjects. I have traveled to several wonderful places because I enjoy learning about other cultures. I even watch public television."

"That doesn't mean you know everything about everything. I admit that you are knowledgeable about things most people could care less about. But, you wouldn't scare people away, or bore them to death if you occasionally asked their opinion."

At that point, we mutually decided we should head back home. The original plan was to stop for dinner someplace along the way, but I said I had a headache and asked to be dropped off at my apartment instead. We shared a quick kiss, and I rode the elevator up to the third floor wondering if this would be the last time I would see Cory. It then dawned on me that Cory had several pieces of clothing in my hall closet, shaving paraphernalia in my bathroom, and a bathrobe hanging on a hook on my bedroom door. I had given Cory a key to the building and my apartment in case he decided to come over when I wasn't home, but I was hoping we could come to an understanding and continue our friendship. I guess I was just going to have to wait and see how long it would take Cory to call me. I know I wasn't going to call him. I felt like a teenager who had just returned my boyfriend's class ring that I had worn on a chain around my neck for the past six months.

I was hoping after a few days went by one of us would grow up and extend an olive branch to the other. I just had to wait and see. I remember the situation did work itself out, and we continued our relationship. Thinking about it now, I had never considered Cory could have been so mad at me he would kill me. He did have keys to my building and apartment, so he could show up anytime he wanted. Naw.

Chapter 17
Penelope True-May

One of my most vivid memories is of a woman that moved into Eden Estates about a year after I did and was definitely a horse of a different color. She reigned from London, England but had lived in the states for the past 45 years. She had fallen in love with an American businessman working in London for an American company, and when he returned to the US, it was with a British bride in tow.

Penelope True-May was tall with red hair that was sprinkled with natural white highlights that looked like they were professionally added to highlight her face. She had striking features including deep green eyes and a ram-rod straight spine. No one could believe she was old enough to live in an apartment building that catered to seniors over the age of 62. She retained dimples in her cheeks that I imagine worked miracles with that long-ago soldier and anyone else of the male persuasion.

I loved her accent and enjoyed listening to her tell stories about her life in England and what it was like to build a new life in America with her new husband, Victor.

Penelope began, "We were very much in love, and I didn't believe that our life in America would be very different than the one we lived in London. Oh, I was so naive. I was probably blinded by my love for Victor and would have been happy living anywhere with him."

We would pump Penelope for facts about London, and she said one time, "Windsor Castle has the distinction of being the longest occupied castle in Europe having been built in the eleventh century. It is still possible for tourists to get close enough for pictures during the week when the monarchy is in residence elsewhere in England, but never on the weekends if the royals are in attendance. There are two different flags that fly over the castle — one if the Queen is in residence and a different one if she isn't."

We asked her about things we had heard about England, and she was happy to verify what was true and what wasn't. Penelope said it was indeed true that the Queen Mother's face was printed on every sheet of toilet paper in every loo in England. She also said that the Royal Family was not allowed to stroll around the castle whenever they wanted. They were barred from going down to the kitchen to get a midnight snack even if they were hungry. And the meals were planned for them, so if they wanted fried chicken, they had to put up with duck under glass instead if that was on the daily menu card. She made it clear being a royal was not all it was cracked up to be.

Many of us were very interested in these discussions, but because they did not include things happening around our building or about people in our building, several people were not interested in what Penelope had to say. I heard Carol say one time, "Why should we care what happens in Europe when we can't take care of the poor people here?" Again, she did not get the point that everything was not about her.

Another woman heard us talking and said, "She don't sound like no Brit I ever heard. She talks English just as good as me."

I said, "What do you expect her to say? Chip-chip cheerio? She has been here for more than fifty years, and because she is intelligent, I would have expected her to lose some of the King's English dialect and adapt to many of the American ways of speaking. Did you know Penelope also speaks French and German?"

Carol just turned her back and started walking out of the room. I heard her say under her breath, "Who cares?"

One afternoon Penelope was at the mailbox when I went to retrieve my bills and junk mail, and we decided to go have coffee. There were about ten others in the community room, so we sat at a table away from the rest.

"Penelope, what was your life in England like? Do you mind talking about it?'

"No, that is fine. I like when people are interested in my life. I know how you feel about it, because I'm very interested in people from other countries also. I'm a very curious person, so when I find out that someone is from a totally different culture than myself, I like asking them about their life."

I asked Penelope, "Where did you actually grow up? I mean, I know it was somewhere in England, but where exactly?"

Penelope looked at her lap for a few moments and then looking into my eyes said, "I had a very unusual childhood that followed into my young adulthood. My family was part of what were called Travelers. We traveled from town to town in our wagons that made up a caravan. We would sell our wares and do odd jobs to earn money. Most of the men in our community could fix anything mechanical or build almost anything out of wood. If the women could find a place to sell their crafts and handmade goods and the men could get a job fixing machines around the village, we might stay for a few weeks or even months. Usually, we didn't stay longer than that because some people were afraid of anyone different than themselves and would start to make trouble for us. Any time there was a problem in the village, we were asked to leave because they thought it must have been related to us."

Nancy was obviously eavesdropping because all of a sudden she spoke up and shouted from the across the room, "You mean you were gypsies. Gypsies can't be trusted. They believe in doing anything to make money, even if it is illegal. They say they can tell the future, but they just make stuff up to make people happy. They are a despicable group of people."

I asked Nancy where she picked up this bit of information. She said she had seen it on Facebook and that everyone knew that everything on Facebook was true.

"Nancy, you can't believe about 90% of what you read on social networks. Everyone knows that."

Carol turned away in a huff, and I continued my conversation with Penelope.

"I am sorry about that. There are some people around here who think they know everything about everything. Did you go to school when you were a child?" I asked.

"We were home-schooled before it became popular. One time we found a very accommodating village that appreciated our skills, and we decided to settle down on the edge of town and put down roots for a time. My parents thought it would be a good idea to send me and my brother to the village school so we could get to know some of the other children and experience their learning methods. When we were tested to determine which level we should be placed in, we both tested three years older than we were. I was supposed to be in level three, but they put me in mid-school. My little brother was enrolled in level five. Because we had been raised to be independent and think for ourselves, we were also much more mature than our classmates. Trevor and I loved school. We had never been in a school with actual textbooks, a library where we could pour over as many books as we could carry home, and recess where we played with the other children. Most of the people in Moorewood Crossing were very nice, and we actually made friends outside of our caravan. Many of the women taught others how to sew, helped them make beautiful quilts, and string their own beads. My dad helped a man build a walkway to his new out-building, and they invited us to a picnic in their yard with some of their neighbors. It was lots of fun, but that night I had a feeling this wasn't going to last long. One of the things we usually kept from the villagers was that we could tell fortunes and see the future. When my mother mentioned something to a woman she knew, she had a bad feeling about the next few days when the woman just gave her funny looks, but didn't say anything. Two days later, the chemist's shop was burgled and burned to the ground. All of a sudden, we were not welcome in Moorewood Crossing any longer and were driven out of town even when it turned out to be the minister's son who had committed the crime. It was a hard lesson for us after we had learned to like the villagers and had grown to trust them. It was a very long time until we went down that road again."

"As I grew up, the popularity of Renaissance fairs grew and grew. What we did for a living fit right into the atmosphere of the fair. We were able to rent a booth at a big event near London, and we made money selling homemade capes and other costumes. We also braided hair and told fortunes. The men worked in the shop. We made more money in that one summer than we had ever made in any other year. As a small community, we took a vote and decided to stay in the area and continue to build a bigger booth with beds in the back and a real bathroom. Because we had made a good bit of money that first summer, we rented a few apartments and were able to buy materials to build up our stock for the next summer. We were no longer nomads, and it changed the way we lived."

"That is where I met Victor. He and some friends came to the fair. I was immediately attracted to him, and I have to say that he felt the same way about me. Victor came to the fair every weekend, and we started having lunch together when I took breaks. We became closer and closer and started seeing each other during the week as well. When Victor received word that he was going to be recalled back to the states, he asked me to marry him and go to America with him. I was so much in love that I really gave no thought about how much my life was going to change. Victor and I married and set off on a brand- new life in the states."

Nancy approached the table I was sharing with Penelope and said, "Are you really a US citizen? How are we going to know for sure? What happened to your husband? Did he also start robbing people and selling what he stole? Maybe he is still alive, and you are pretending to be a widow. Is the plan to start stealing from all of us at Eden Estates and then leave in the middle of the night with the loot? I can't wait to tell everyone about you, you, you, you gypsy."

I could not contain my anger. I looked at Penelope, and it was obvious she knew what a fruitcake Nancy was and did not take anything she said seriously.

I said, "Have you taken a look around here lately, Nancy? Most of us don't have two cents to rub together let alone have treasures piled inside of our apartments that people would be willing to kill for. Do you think your 30-year-old Precious Moments figurines are worth anything? You can buy them in any antique store for three or four dollars apiece. I haven't seen anyone walking around in mink coats or wearing diamond and ruby necklaces. Just leave Penelope alone and go mind your own business."

Chapter 18
Two Special Men

A couple of men in my building had been very nice. There was Nick Olson, the maintenance man, and Jeff Newman, the caretaker.

Nick was so kind to all of us and would readily help us in ways that were not included in his job description. When I got my new license plates for my car, I pulled my tool box out of the closet and set it down in back of my car. I chose a screwdriver I thought would easily remove four screws from the license plates. I was wrong. I continued to try to remove the screws until my hand screamed out in pain. Nick came by, saw me struggling with the task, and asked if he could assist me. I acquiesced and allowed him to tackle the problem. Even he had trouble with the screws because they were rusted in place. Nick went to his car and retrieved a much larger tool box with a lot more screwdrivers to choose from. He selected one with the ability to push on the screw to get them loose. It took Nick about fifteen minutes to remove my old license plates and replace them with the new, shiny ones. I offered to give him some money, but he declined the offer and just walked away smiling. I know it made him happy to help us old ladies out, and I could just imagine how he might go home at night to share with his wife the funny things he had helped us out with. We could be a very funny bunch when we had a hard time completing a task because many of us became frustrated when we realized we needed help with almost everything we tried to repair. This was just another fact I had to come to grips with as I grew older and tried to deny at every turn.

On more than one occasion, I needed someone to look at a problem in my apartment, and Nick always made time to check it out. There were certain people in the building who seemed to take up a lot of his time, but he was helpful and polite to all of us. For instance, over a period of time, the water in my shower was not getting very hot, and when Nick heard me mention it to another resident who I was having coffee with, he came over to the table and asked me about it. When I explained the situation, he said he could go right up and look at it if I wanted and felt comfortable with him going into my apartment without me being there. I told him I would appreciate anything he could do. He came back about twenty minutes later and said all he had to do was replace a worn-out valve, and my shower was now putting out steaming hot water again. While he was there, he also checked that the faucets did not drip and the handles were secure.

I had heard horror stories from some friends that live in apartment buildings where they have a horrible time getting anything fixed. I felt grateful we had Nick.

I also liked the fact that Nick treated all the seniors in the building with dignity and respect. He patiently listened to all our "in-the-good-old-days" stories and asked questions about our families. He mentioned he had never had an aunt, so being around us made him feel like he had several. Sometimes we would offer him coffee or tea if he was in our apartments making repairs. We all knew he enjoyed the occasional piece of cake or a couple of cookies when he was working. Nick reminded a lot of us of the sons we either never had, or ones who lived far away so our access to them was limited. He was funny and trustworthy; it was nice having him around, and I always took up a collection at Christmas time so we could put a nice surprise in his holiday card to show him our appreciation. He could have not been nicer.

Jeff was also very nice and worked hard keeping the building clean and comfortable. Jeff was often seen cleaning the tables in the community room, vacuuming the hallways, dusting the window ledges and polishing the furniture. He was also happy to help some of us put up the Christmas tree in the community room, including stringing the lights. He had a great sense of humor and enjoyed telling jokes to anyone who would listen.

One time, Jeff helped me clean my ceiling fan blades, and when daylight savings time made us reset our clocks, he changed mine in the kitchen. Because I am short, he didn't want me climbing up on my countertops to do it myself. He did many small tasks like this, and everyone (well, almost everyone) in the building was happy and thankful for Jeff.

If there were just a few people in the community room while he was cleaning, we would ask him how his weekend or holiday went. He was always happy to share with us the adventures he had with his grandchildren. Jeff was happiest when he was spending time with his family.

After he had taken a vacation to Disney World one winter with his family, he brought ~~the~~ pictures to share with us. He looked so happy riding in the teacups with his granddaughter and on the train with his grandson. He said he had a hard time coming back to the cold weather in Wisconsin after spending time in 80-degree weather in Florida. We told him we were thankful he returned.

Chapter 19
The Garden

I was told that in past years, there had been beautiful flowers planted in several large clay pots lining the covered patio. Not only did they improve the aesthetics of the plain, three-story, brick building, but the residents enjoyed the beauty, colors, and textures of the different flowers. They liked watching them grow from small bedding plants into lush, aromatic specimens. When spring came around, I took it upon myself to ask the manager if we could request some funds in order to purchase plants, black dirt, and a few smaller, colorful pots to put between the large ones.

Linda, the building manager, said, "I will ask the company if that's possible. I think I can get you about $50, but probably not any more than that."

I asked her if she would have a problem if I took up a collection from the residents to cover the cost of anything over the $50 they would supply. She did not see why that wouldn't work if I was willing to take on that task, along with buying, planting, and caring for the plants. I had really missed working in my garden with my hands in the dirt and planning what to plant. The selection would depend on how much sun the pots would enjoy during the day. I was ecstatic. I was really excited at the prospect of finally doing some gardening, if you could call it that. I put notes up in the elevator and on the bulletin board, the accepted method for getting the word out about anything that concerned all the residents in the building. Not everyone took the elevator, but all of us came to the mailboxes each day, and they were located next to the bulletin board.

The notice stated, "*I will be taking contributions for plants to go into the large pots on the patio. I would appreciate anything you are willing to donate. You can give the money directly to me or just slip an envelope underneath my door. Any amount will be appreciated. Thanks, Betty*"

As word spread, I received cash donations of large and small amounts from several people who were delighted we would again have a beautiful patio. They would be proud to show off their home when friends and relatives came to visit or pick them up in the front of the building.

When I had collected $100 both from the manager and the residents, I shopped for plants at several nurseries and building supply stores to get the best prices. Some of the people who gave me money had requested certain plants, and I did my best to appease as many people as I could, given the confines of the money I had to spend.

The next day Tootsie helped me unload the many flats of flowers I had purchased and prepare the pots for planting. There were sticks and rocks we had to remove to add new potting soil where needed. After that I was tired and decided to put off the planting until the next day.

When some of the residents went down to the community room for coffee the next morning, and saw the planters had not been filled, they were complaining because they couldn't understand why I hadn't finished the job I had started the day before.

Marianne entered the community room and took a seat with her only two friends in the building. She scrunched up her face until she resembled Oscar the Grouch and commented, "I don't like the plants you chose. I would have picked nicer plants and different colors. You wasted our money."

I said, "That statement would mean more coming from someone who had actually contributed money to pay for the plants." The complainers did not like that the only people who would make decisions about the planting were the ones who had contributed to the cost or provided the labor. I said, "Marianne, if you put as much energy into doing the work as you do complaining, we would be done already. And if you would help us do the planting, you could get some fresh air and exercise. Who knows, you may even be able to work off some of your love handles by doing some much needed physical labor." I heard several snickers and some polite applause. Marianne and her cohorts left the community room in a huff. Again. I believe she doesn't know any other way to leave a room, with a scowl on her face and scrunched-up shoulders. I wonder if Marianne realized all of wrinkles that were formed when she was mad might turn out to be permanent.

I looked at the rest of the people and said, "If anyone wants to help me plan and plant the pots, I would really appreciate it. Moving large bags of dirt, digging out the pots to make room for the plants and doing all the planting is more than a one-woman job." I was pleased that Audrey, JoAnne, and Tootsie said if I would wait for them to go get their gardening gloves, they would love to have a say in what the patio would look like when we were finished.

I was glad that the negative people would not be around to critique my every move, and every decision would be made by me and my helpers. We spent the rest of the day with our hands in the dirt planting not only the large pots on the patio but several smaller ones left over from years past. When we were finished, there was a riot of colors, shapes, sizes, and textures spilling from the pots. Stepping back and admiring our work was very rewarding. After we had watered the plants and cleaned up the patio of garden tools and left over dirt, we entered the community room to shouts of wonder and happy people thanking us for our hard work. They commented how much we would all enjoy watching these plants grow and display their color for the entire summer. I decided it was all worth the time and effort to see so many people express joy in our handiwork.

There was a similar situation concerning the bird feeders. Tootsie and I were the only ones collecting money for the bird food, buying the suet and bird seed to keep the feeders full every day. Even though everyone remarked how entertaining it was watching the birds playing in the bird bath and eating the bird seed, it didn't dawn on most of them to help out once in a while. Tootsie and I continued to do it because we loved the birds and how much they enjoyed the feast we offered them each day. I guess you could say that we were doing it for ourselves and if we could give the others something to feel good about, it was all worth it.

Chapter 20
The Field Trip

A few weeks later, Audrey called and said, "Some of the women are planning to go on a field trip so we can get away from here for a while. Two of our friends have seen a posting in the local paper about an outing offered to seniors. We would take a bus from the community center to an old train station about an hour away and then board a dining car, circa 1930."

Because it was summer time, the trip to the train station was a beautiful one. The trees were bursting with bright, beautiful leaves and the wild flowers in fields we passed were rejuvenating. We also saw many barns with quilt patterns painted on them, and there were never two alike.

The dining car was luxuriously appointed, and we felt like we had stepped back in time to when travelers were treated like royalty as they lounged in comfortable chairs and were indulged with a beautifully set table featuring linen table cloths and napkins. There were interesting patterns being displayed on the table as the sun came shining through the trees. The food was delectable, the atmosphere was quaint, and riding along through a wooded area made us all feel we were being treated to a luxurious experience.

The old dining car we were in made us all nostalgic about good times in our past. We started sharing our own memories about wonderful times in our own lives. Lillian was reminiscing about a time that was particularly memorable. The clickity-clack of the wheels on the track just added to the atmosphere.

Lillian shared, "My dad worked on the railroad when I was a child, and sometimes he was given free passes to ride the train. Once, we went to Chicago for a long weekend and stayed in an actual hotel — something we had only seen in the movies and certainly never done before. We rode in a taxi, also a first, and walked around the downtown loop admiring the very tall buildings where the sky looked like a ribbon of blue between the skyscrapers. I miss doing things like that and wish I had the finances to take even short trips."

JoAnne reminisced about how she and her husband had gone to Niagara Falls on their honeymoon and had gotten soaking wet because they wandered too close to the edge. "That was the last time we went near any waterfalls." She missed her husband of 48 years terribly and felt she had been depressed for a long time. That was another reason this sort of activity was good for all of us.

I shared with my friends that I was thinking about how great it would have been to share this experience with Larry. "But honestly, I can't see Larry on this train. He was not a very adventurous sort, and he was happy to putter around in his wood shop, watch TV, and spend afternoons on the driving range. We even kept company with the same four couples we had known for over forty years. It was always the same conversations that took place among some of the men. The women would sit around the kitchen table and discuss our health issues, politics, vacations, our kids and grandkids, and our plans for next spring's garden".

When everyone left, and I was cleaning up the kitchen, I told Larry about my visit with the women. "Did Brian tell you his son has been accepted at MIT? Susan is so excited for him. And isn't it sad that Vernon's cancer has come back? That has to be very scary for him and Nancy. Did Carl tell you that he and Theresa are going on a European cruise next year? Oh, how I envy them. "What did you and the men talk about?"

Larry looked bored, "We are all happy to be retired so we can work on our hobbies. Brian told us all about golfing with the Governor, and we discussed the weather — how unusual it is to get this much rain this time of year."

My belief that Larry was wasting his retirement remained intact after listening to my husband's retelling of what transpired between the other men. They wouldn't talk about their feelings if their lives depended on it. Men!

Chapter 21
Things to Consider

If I was going to ever find out who hated me so much, I had to be really honest with myself and examine my part in this tragedy.

First of all, there was Marianne. I had several run-ins with her, and I couldn't stop myself from taking advantage of her ignorance about most topics we normally discussed in the community room. I didn't even care that I was embarrassing her in front of everyone. I wondered if I had been a bully. Thinking back, I had not treated some of my neighbors with the dignity and respect I wanted from them. Sometimes I gave no thought to what they were feeling. Why did I need to always push my agenda no matter the cost? Right there I had several suspects for doing me in.

I know I needed to be much more watchful to everything people were saying about me and what had transpired. Having the ability to spy on them when they had no idea I was still present was a definite asset. I just wish I could have been a better person when it really mattered. If I had acted with integrity and respectfully, I may still be alive.

Since I did not know the cause of my death, and had no memory of what had happened before I found myself in the dumpster, I needed to be very attentive to everything going on at Eden Estates. I hung around the community room quite a bit because that was the major communication area in the building.

Politics and religion were topics to be avoided and rarely took place unless everyone in the room at the time was of the same belief. But everything else was discussed at length, and many times it was exactly the same dialog that had taken place the day before. Be it health problems, money issues, family troubles, all the residents had something to offer. It did not surprise me that people who had more past than future would rehash time and again the amazing stories that this population had lived. When people reach the age of 80 or 90 years, they could tell me stories I never learned about in history books. This rich fabric of people's lives had been fascinating to me, and I enjoyed most of my time in the community room. Naturally, there were exceptions to every rule.

When Marianne and her posse appeared, almost everyone ignored them and continued their visiting. After hearing my experiences with her, they finally recognized it was up to them to either give in to her ranting or just ignore her completely. Marianne was a bully and a blowhard, but she actually had no power over us so she came down to the community room less and less.

I needed to find a way for this investigation to move forward, and I was going to need help. If I could find a way to make people open up among themselves, maybe it would supply me with the evidence I was missing.

I forgot that I couldn't be seen or heard by the other people and sneaked around stealthily. When I remembered my invisibility, I began playing games with them. I would walk through their bodies and watch them shiver, float around their heads, hang around the laundry room and watch them talk to themselves. I learned a lot about the residents in this manner, more than if they were in the company of others.

Once, Joyce was folding clothes in the third floor laundry room, and I heard her mumble to herself that she was really sick of Lillian hogging all the coffee creamer. "You would think someone her age would realize when the cream is running low, and she shops for groceries twice a week, she might think to replace at least what she used. How can she be so selfish? I can't be the only person here who has noticed her greed."

Now, this was something I had never thought to pay attention to — people taking to themselves! I didn't have to wait until they were speaking to another tenant, I could listen in on conversations they were having with themselves. Yippee! A new avenue to explore.

I next went down to float around the mailboxes because when the mail carrier came, there would be a crowd making all kinds of comments. The usual suspects were gathered there and already complaining about what they thought they would receive today in the mail. I called these individuals the "pre-complainers."

Elaine watched the others like they were all crazy. I liked Elaine. When she was joined by a friend, Lillian, they started whispering about the "incident" that happened to me.

"Can you believe anyone would take such extreme measures to do away with Betty?" Lillian asked. "I know she could be a little opinionated but, really! Obviously, it was someone who had a hard time confronting someone like Betty who stuck up for herself."

Elaine answered, "I heard she was shot, but nobody heard a gunshot, so I guess it must have been just a rumor. I wonder what really happened?"

Elaine asked Lillian, "Who do you think was responsible and how did they do it?"

Lillian said, "I heard she was strangled with a drapery cord, although, everyone here has those mini-blinds in their apartments, not drapes. Genevieve said she overheard two people talking in the elevator. They said Betty had been very mean to Marianne."

"Betty was mean to Marianne? You know Marianne is the worst possible neighbor in the building. She bullies everyone about everything. I think Marianne deserved what she got from Betty because she brought it on herself. Betty also stuck up for others when Marianne was around. I think Betty was a nice person."

It was nice to hear someone siding with me, even now. But, I wasn't looking for the people who liked me, just the ones who hated me. The search went on.

I thought it was time to spy on Marianne and her friends. They happened to be congregating on the patio right now.

"Marianne, you know that everyone thinks you killed Betty, don't you?" said Alice.

"Yes, I guess I do, but I don't care."

Donna spoke up, "You will care if the police start asking you questions, and you don't have the right answers. Look at all the things that people here can tell them, all of the times you were mean to Betty or her friends. Doesn't that scare you? Because if it doesn't, it should."

"Shut up, Alice. You must have been intimidated by Betty too. What can she do to you now? She can never make trouble for any of us again. Just keep your mouth closed, and if the cops question you, make sure you defend me and make Betty the bully. Got it?"

Alice said, "I will not defend you. If the police question me, I will tell them the truth."

Marianne just gave her normal growl as she scowled at Alice.

Chapter 22
Lunch Appointment

I remembered back to a time when JoAnn and I had a standing appointment to have lunch every Thursday. JoAnn did not drive, so I knew she really appreciated knowing that at least once a week she would be able to get out and have some fun. In repayment, she insisted she pick up the check for our lunches.

One day, a very annoying person named Carol Carlson invited herself along without being asked. There was a fly in the ointment, however. When Carol told me she would be going with us she announced, "I have to ride in the front seat because I get car sick sitting in the back."

I thought I had better alert JoAnn to the change of plans. I called and told her what Carol had said. JoAnn was furious. She really lost it and shouted into the telephone, "How could Carol not only invite herself to our lunch, but say that she needed to sit in the front seat? She knows I need to ride in the front because she has seen me get car sick riding in the back of a car."

I told JoAnne she and Carol would have to work it out themselves and that it didn't matter to me who rode where. After JoAnn talked to Carol, she called me back. "Well, thanks for sticking up for me" she said. "Since neither of us can ride in the back, we decided that both of us are staying home. You should have told Carol these luncheons are very important to me and she simply could not butt in and invite herself."

That was the end of that outing. Once again, when I tried to do something nice for someone I ended up getting blamed when it didn't turn out well. There seemed to have been many situations like that in the last year. I don't know how I got myself into the middle of so many problems between other people. I replayed another of these situations in my head.

Angela Brown was a wonderful woman. With a kind personality and a giving nature, she was always willing to help out when we were planning an event for the building. She had several good suggestions about things we could do to make Eden Estates more fun for everyone. Angela was a crafter's crafter. She could do anything: knit, crochet, beading, play the piano, and bake wonderful desserts that she shared with everyone. I thought she was a huge asset to the building.

One time she organized a "Friday Breakfast" where each week people would make something having to do with breakfast and bring it down to the community room for all to share. At first there were only a couple of us who took part, but as the word spread, more and more people became interested and joined the festivities. Each week there was much more variety with different items. Elaine made wonderful, huge, puffy popovers, and we slathered them with tons of butter. YUM! No matter how many she made, there were never any leftovers. That was one of my favorite items on the table.

JoAnn was known for her quiches and usually made two or three different kinds. These were all made by hand and the crusts melted in our mouths. Sharp cheddar cheese, real bacon, sautéed onions and fresh eggs combined to make a delectable treat.

Others brought the normal items like toast, scrambled eggs and sausage links. All in all, Friday was our favorite day of the week for all who participated.

Chapter 23
The Patio

Several of us were enjoying a beautiful fall day sitting on the covered patio on the south side of the building. There were three patio tables with matching chairs and several other chairs in small groupings. One end of the patio was a designated smoking area with a park bench and an ashtray. There were about five smokers who lived in the building.

One man was as reliable as Big Ben. Every hour, on the hour, Walt Waterson would shuffle out the door and over to one specific chair next to the ash tray. He didn't talk much, but listened very carefully to everyone that was speaking. We became so immune to his presence, he seemed to just disappear into the scenery, which made some people speak out of turn about delicate issues around the place. As far as I knew, he never repeated what he heard but just stored it away somewhere in that brain of his. I wondered if he would ever use what he learned against another resident.

Norma Simpson, now she was another case altogether. She also sat in the same place every day but never wanted anyone to sit in the chair beside her. I guess she had a thing about privacy. Norma would give her opinions about any subject being discussed but never took advice that was sent her way.

Angela was relaying a time when she had to work three jobs in order to support her kids after her husband left when the girls were seven and nine years old. "After spending eight hours behind a desk," she said, "I would either go to another office to do data entry for three to four hours or go to work at a little café near my home. I only had one night off a week from my second job and some Sundays to spend with my kids." Angela spoke softly and almost to herself, "I was not sure we would make it from one week 'til the next. A lot of my money came from tips, and if the café wasn't busy, I could make as little as $3.00 a night. When I got home at eight or nine at night, the girls and I would read books or play gin rummy until it was time for them to go to bed. I felt guilty all the time, but I had to make a tough decision when their no-good dad left with the town slut. I could either go on welfare or work like a dog to keep us together. I never received a dime from their father 'cause no one ever knew where he went to, he just vanished. It was hard on me and the girls," Angela went on, "but there was some good that came out if that terrible time. My girls learned that nothin' in this world is free, so you have to work as hard as you can at whatever job you can get. It also taught 'em to be independent very young and to solve problems when I wasn't 'round to help. One of the biggest regrets was I couldn't put my kids in dancin' class like the other girls or have 'em play music 'cause I couldn't lay out good money for extra stuff and then find out I couldn't pay the rent."

With a cigarette dangling from her mouth Norma sneered, "You don't know nothing about working hard until your hands bleed, and you can't stand up straight 'cause your back was almost broke. When you don't get your welfare check on time, and you gotta do dirty, back-breaking jobs for cash just to put food on the table, now that is a bad time."

I spoke up to defend Angela, "Norma, just because you chose to live on welfare and Angela decided to work her butt off instead is no reason to put her down."

I thought Norma was going to come right out of her chair and attack me. "Why, you're nothin' but white trash, and a nigger lovin' bitch. You got no right to judge me. You and your highfalutin' life in lily white Iowa where you didn't have all them black people was a cake walk. You don't know what you are talking about. They made the gov'ment pay for college and then took all the good jobs from us poor white folk." Norma was red as a beet and almost frothing at the mouth. For a minute, I thought she was going to have a stroke.

I shared with her what Angela had told me a few days ago, "Norma, Angela's kids studied very hard in high school, so they did receive some scholarship money from their colleges, but mainly they paid for their education with student loans, like everyone else, which took them several years to repay. So, the truth is they did get help from the government, but never a handout. Your kids could have done the same thing if they wanted to get ahead, but I don't suppose you even gave them that choice."

Genevieve, who never wanted anyone to be upset, patted Norma on the back and brought her a glass of water. Norma was still breathing hard when I ask Angela if she would like to go inside and have a cup of coffee. We left Norma and the others on the patio. You could almost hear a pin drop.

I was surprised that through this whole confrontation, Marianne didn't speak up to say her piece or give anyone advice. I think she was so blown away that she couldn't think of anything to say. That had to be a first. Neither of her friends spoke up either, but that was business as usual. If Marianne didn't talk, they didn't dare open their mouths.

Another time, several people were again sitting on the patio talking about different vacations they had taken or were planning to with their families. Nancy was telling us that her son's family was going to take her to Washington DC to celebrate her 85th birthday. They would be gone for ten days in the spring during the celebrated cherry blossom time. Tootsie ask, "What things do you want to see most in Washington?"

"Well, most of all I want to see the White House. Donny has tickets for all of us to go on a guided tour. We will do that on the first day, and then we will spend a couple of days visiting monuments and museums. My granddaughter is really excited about spending some time at the Smithsonian, so we will probably be there for a couple of days too. I want to see the Vietnam Memorial because I have two sons and a nephew who died during that war, and I want to find their names and make rubbings. I will bring them home and put them in a frame along with pictures of them in their uniforms." Nancy got quiet for a few minutes, and we let her have her moment. "Anyway," she said, "We will then go to Philadelphia to see the Liberty Bell and other sites. I am really excited because this may be the last trip I take."

JoAnn said she had also been to Washington and had enjoyed it a lot. However, her favorite vacation was when her sister and brother-in-law took her on a Caribbean cruise a few years ago. "It was so wonderful going to all of those islands. One of the best times was going to the beach on St. Maarten. We collected shells and went swimming on the white sand beach. The tour also included a very nice lunch and time to shop. I always get a Christmas ornament for a souvenir wherever I go. They are usually small and easy to pack, so when I put up my tree in December, it brings back all kinds of wonderful memories of my trips. We saw something different on each island we visited, and I took many, many wonderful pictures. That is half the fun for me, putting together photo albums of my trips because then I can revisit the wonderful time I had any time I want to."

JoAnn asked me what my favorite vacation was, and I agree with her. A cruise was my favorite also. I really loved the entertainment, food, and shopping on the ship and watching the beautiful sunsets we had each night. One time I was able to see the little "green flash" I had heard about. The very second the sun goes beneath the horizon you might see a really fast green light. We watched very carefully from our cabin's deck and did not even blink, because it happens so fast. Most people never get to see the flash, so it was a nice touch to end a wonderful day we had spent touring St. Lucia.

Lorraine was telling us about a time when she and a few friends went to Alaska in the summertime. She was describing the beautiful icebergs and polar bears when Maureen came out to the patio and plunked herself right down in the middle of the group. She interrupted Lorraine by asking, "I wonder what the weather is going to be tomorrow."

JoAnn was nice enough to pull out her cell phone and check the weather. "It is going to be 75 and sunny tomorrow," she announced.

Lorraine continued telling about her wonderful adventure until Maureen said again, "I wonder what the weather is going to be like tomorrow." JoAnn told her again that it was going to be 75 and sunny.

Lorraine continued speaking about Alaska for about five more minutes. Others chimed in about vacations they had enjoyed and everyone liked hearing about other people's adventures. For the third time, Maureen interrupted, "Does anyone know what the weather is going to be like tomorrow?"

I had enough. I gave Maureen a dirty look and asked her if she had not heard the answers about the weather each time she had asked. "Well, you don't have to treat me like I am stupid," Maureen said.

I told her," If you would quit asking stupid questions, we would quit giving you the same answers." Everyone kind of squirmed in their chairs, but I knew they had wished they had said something like that to Maureen also.

JoAnn looked at me and asked if I wanted to go to Trader Joe's. I shook my head in a positive manner, and we got up to leave. As we walked away Maureen said very pointedly, "Goodbye, JoAnn." She was evidently so mad at me she didn't even want to speak to me. I could live with that, or so I thought.

When I returned from the store, my phone in my purse started ringing as soon as I put my key in the lock. I hurriedly opened the door and dropped my packages on the floor so I could answer my phone. "Hello, hello," I said without looking at the caller ID.

"Betty," Maureen said. "Why don't you like me?"

Oh, the scenarios that ran through my mind. However, I thought I should be truthful and at the same time try to be as kind as I could. "Maureen," I began. "It isn't that I don't like you, but when you come into a group that is having a conversation and interrupt to ask a question that has nothing to do with the subject at hand, it is very disturbing. JoAnn told you three times what the weather would be tomorrow, and you continued to ask again and again. We were talking about our experiences on vacations, and the weather was not being discussed. Does that make sense to you?"

"Well, I just wanted to know what the weather was going to be tomorrow, and I don't remember asking more than once."

"Do you understand why people get angry with you when you ask all kinds of questions about them and what they are doing, even though it is none of your business? You have asked me what the doctor told me when I return from my appointments. You have asked me if I was playing cards when you came over to the table where six of us were playing cards. It's like you never notice what is going on around you and then ask stupid questions over and over and over."

Maureen stopped talking for about thirty seconds and then asked me. "But why don't you like me?"

I told her I gave up trying to be friends with her, and I wish she would just stay away from me from now on, and hung up.

I couldn't believe it when ten minutes later she came and knocked on my door. Thankfully, I looked through the peephole and declined to open the door when I saw her standing there. She could hear my TV and said, "I know you are in there. Please let me in so we can talk. I need to know why you don't like me." She must have stood there for five minutes and continued to knock on the door. She finally left. Good riddance, I thought. That is finally over. And it was over until I went to the mailbox the next day. Maureen was sitting in a chair next to Tootsie and was saying, "I just don't know why Betty doesn't like me." I felt sorry for Tootsie, but I turned on the stairs and scurried back up to the third floor before Maureen could spot me. I was worried I would never be able to leave my apartment again.

Chapter 24
The Food Shelf

Another possible confrontation that I just remembered was when the food shelf came to the building. On the first and third week of each month, the local food shelf brought food to anyone who had placed an order that week. Each person received what they had ordered plus a lot of other items that filled up two or three grocery bags. There were normally three or four items that were placed on tables in the entryway that anyone could take, even if they had not placed an order that week. Normally, it was some type of cheese, yogurt, fruits and vegetables in season, or bread. The people who had placed an order would get first pick of the extra items and then the rest of us were invited to choose what we wanted.

Carol was a person who took advantage of the extra items and so much more. Even before she had been called to get her order, she went out into the foyer to help herself to the extra items. Then a friend of hers asked if she would pick up some of the extra items because they were having problems walking. When Carol was gathering the items her friend wanted, she also took more for herself. After she had examined what was in her cart, she went to the others who had also received groceries and looked through their carts. If she saw something she wanted, she would ask that person if she could have it. Most people did not want to refuse Carol anything she wanted because she could be really mean if she didn't get her way (she and Marianne were friends). Carol would pile her cart to overflowing and then go back to the foyer where the extra food was waiting for the other residents. She would grab as much as she could hold and add it to her cart even before anyone else had a chance to see what was there.

Tootsie had witnessed this several times and finally had enough. She looked at all of the cheese sticks in Carol's hands and said, "Carol, you have been through this line three times and most people have not even been through once. How greedy can you get? Are you really going to eat all of the food you take or are you just going to hoard it like you do everything else?"

Carol was shocked that someone would confront her and gave Tootsie a dirty look before she returned to the community room where she started telling everyone that Tootsie was mean and she never did anything for anyone. "Miss high and mighty, who does she think she is?" Everyone looked at Carol like she was crazy. They knew what a wonderful, thoughtful, helpful person Tootsie was so they knew it was just Carol blowing off steam. They were also familiar with Carol's personality and her habit of making trouble for anyone who crossed her.

I seem to remember that as time went on, Carol alienated most of the people in the building, including the manager. She would spread lies about anyone she disliked and didn't care whose toes she was stepping on. Carol was an enigma — on one hand, she didn't care who she insulted yet she went out of her way to find people to be friends with. The problem was that she was so two-faced, nobody could possibly trust her so even with most of her "friends" not one of them could be counted on to come to her aid or go out of their way to defend her.

As far as Tootsie was concerned, this altercation with Carol was the last straw. She never spoke to Carol again, and neither did I. I was glad that there were very few people like Carol in the building.

Chapter 25
The Christmas Tree

It had been December, 2015 when the manager had brought a huge box containing an artificial Christmas tree down to the community room. She said it was entirely up to us whether it was even put together. She didn't care because this was for our enjoyment, not hers.

A few of us opened the box and stared at what looked to be a thousand tree branches all flattened out and stuck together. Evidently the people who had taken it down last year just stuffed it into the box any old way just to get it done. There was no thought put into the idea that someone else would have to deconstruct this mess the next year before we could even start putting it together.

Tootsie and I started removing the branches and putting them into piles where the colored ends matched each other. This was a very old type of tree and this is not going to be easy. After we had made piles of branches labeled A through G we started fitting the ends into the correct slots of the metal trunk and spread the branches out to make it look more like an actual tree. It was excruciating slow and evidently only JoAnn, Tootsie, and myself were interested in putting up the Christmas tree, even though there were at least ten people in the room sitting around drinking coffee and offering unasked for advice.

Arleen whispered to JoAnn, "They call that a Christmas tree? When I was a girl the whole family would pile into the car and drive a long way out of the cities to look for a tree. We didn't always end up where we were supposed to go, but we always got our tree. Once, we went to a state forest and found the best tree we ever had. I know it was against the law to cut down a tree in a forest, but my dad said there were millions of them so they would never miss this one."

JoAnn stared at Arleen like she had just told her that her family had started a forest fire. "I can't believe you did that. What if everyone cut down trees in a protected forest?"

"Well, we never got caught, so it doesn't matter. This here tree isn't a Christmas tree. It's just pieces metal with some plastic needles stickin' out of them. Why couldn't they buy a real tree? They're just too cheap. I don't want anything to do with this. I'm going home." No one in the room was sad to see Arleen stomp out of the room mumbling to herself.

JoAnn turned to Tootsie and me and said, "Even if Eden Estates did buy a real tree, there would be a fight about what kind of tree they bought and how big it should be. Some people would object to cutting down a real tree when there are artificial ones that look just like the real thing. Granted, this one is probably twenty years old and is in rough shape, but I appreciate their thoughtfulness."

After the tree was constructed we were trying to find the best side to put in the front, and again ten people with ten different views felt theirs was better than the one we had decided on. We ignored the advice and started hanging the lights.

"I think you have more red ones on the back than you do the front. And there are only four yellow ones on the whole left side. I think you need to spread the white ones out more." This coming from a woman who had never made a pot of coffee or tossed out an empty pie plate. She didn't even clean up her own spilled coffee. There were many people living here who did the same thing. Even if they did not do anything for anyone else or help around the building, they always had advice for those of us that did.

"I like the lights that flash on and off, not the ones that just stay on all the time," Gerry contributed. "Can we play some Christmas music? Not the Twelve Days of Christmas. I hate the Twelve Days of Christmas."

"I want to hear Frank Sinatra songs. He is the best."

"No, he isn't. Perry Como is the best Christmas carol singer."

Everyone in the room had a different idea of who we should be listening to. None of them were the same.

Just then Marianne entered the room. "Oh look, here we have the Christmas elves acting all Christian and happy. It looks like you have decided to put up the tree and decorations." Looking over at the others Marianne said, "That means that Betty and her friends get to decide what our Christmas tree will look like, and we will need to put up with it until January."

"Marianne," I replied," If you would like to help us, you would also be able to decide what the tree and the community room look like."

"Well, all I know is that if I were doing the tree, it would look a whole lot better than this hot mess. The lights are all wrong, the ornaments are ugly, and the decorations on the tables are childish. Do you still believe in Santa Claus?"

I tried to ignore Marianne, took an electric menorah out of another box, and put it on the piano where it was displayed last year. Marianne gave me a revolting look and couldn't help herself from making a snide remark. "Why are you putting that up? It doesn't have anything to do with Christmas."

JoAnn said, "There are five Jewish people living here that celebrate Hanukkah, and we want them to feel welcome to use this room during their holidays, too. It won't hurt you to cooperate
with people of other faiths. This is supposed to be the season of peace and joy not vindictiveness and hate altercation." Somehow, I didn't think so.

Once again, because Marianne couldn't get her way, she stomped out of the room. I wondered if there was going to ever be a time when she and I could be in the same room and not get into an argument.

Chapter 26
Carlton

I kept thinking about the people who had challenges in their lives yet I never heard them complain about anything. One of these people was Carlton Nash. I saw him every day in the community room, at the mailboxes, or outside having a cigarette. Carlton had many health problems including diabetes, heart disease, and walked with a pronounced limp. Carlton was not one to take advantage of his disabilities, however. He often made coffee, unloaded the dishwasher, cleaned off the counter if it was dirty, and never complained about anything. He was a joy to be around. He had a sharp wit and a great sense of humor. He told the worst jokes and then laughed until his eyes watered. His family came to see him often and always brought a treat for everyone in the community room. They would take him grocery shopping every week, and he was known to buy treats for the dogs that lived in the building. Every time the dogs saw Carlton, they would rush to his side for their treat. He made them sit, or dance, or lay down in order to get their reward, and they complied every time. When he would take a dog biscuit out of his pocket and give it to the dogs, they were in heaven. They also knew that they only got one treat a day and left him alone after that.

The only thing about Carlton that people didn't like was that he couldn't keep a secret. Even if you told him something in confidence, he just couldn't help repeating it to whoever would listen. He then would say, "Now don't tell anyone I told you that." It was a well-known fact that if you wanted something spread around the building, you just told Carlton. He would get the word out faster than a telephone. Consequently, everyone looked around to make sure he wasn't around if they wanted to share something private with another person.

Unfortunately for Elaine, either she wasn't aware of or she didn't remember, that telling Carlton something was like taking an ad out in the newspaper. She told him something personal and was shocked that everyone she met around the building asked her about this very intimate information.

I was passing by a sitting area where Carlton and Elaine were having a conversation. They said they were remembering moments in their youth, and then they started speaking very quietly with their heads close together. I assumed they were discussing topics that were of a personal nature, so I kept on walking out to the elevator.

Carlton was a little older than Elaine, but they both were of the same generation and had attended the same schools. Several times I heard them discussing people they had grown up with and usually laughing at remembering their childhood antics. They were still talking when I was returning to my apartment, and I saw them still in the sitting area.

A couple of days later, I saw Elaine speaking with JoAnn, and Elaine was very upset and crying. JoAnn said she felt bad, but she just wanted to say how sorry she was about what happened to Elaine when she was in high school.

Elaine blubbered between sobs, "Nobody was supposed to know about this. I told Carlton because he was going on and on about Robert, a guy we both knew in high school. He was saying what a successful businessman Robert had become, and he was proud that they still kept in touch."

I didn't want to make Elaine feel bad, but I did point out that everyone knew we couldn't trust Carlton to keep a secret. Elaine said she was going to go down to Carlton's apartment and confront him. I didn't think this was a good idea until she had cooled down and gained some composure. But, Elaine was adamant. I asked if I could go with her for moral support, and she said that would be fine. I really wanted to make sure she didn't attack Carlton. I felt that Elaine had a right to speak her feelings I just didn't want any bloodshed. I guess right now that is sort of a funny thing to say considering my current situation.

When we arrived at apartment #123, Elaine knocked at the door. We could hear Carlton approaching, and when the door opened, he smiled at us like he had just invited us to tea. Noticing that Elaine was upset, he looked surprised and asked if he could help her.

"I think you have done enough, Carlton. How could you? How could you? How could you?"

Carlton just stared at Elaine and looked confused. "What have I done? I don't understand why you are so upset with me."

"Did you think for even one minute that what we discussed about Robert was for public disclosure? I told you that in confidence, Carlton. If I wanted everyone to know I had been raped when I was 16 years old, I would have had Linda put it in the monthly newsletter!"

"Oh, I am so sorry. I didn't know that I was the only one you told about it. I assumed you and your women friends here told each other everything."

Elaine shoved Carlton aside and stood by his sofa. Carlton and I followed her into the living room and took a seat. Elaine started pacing around through the kitchen and back to the living room, over and over again. She finally stood right in front of Carlton and glared down at him. "The only reason I told you, Carlton was because you kept going on and on about what a great guy Robert was. You were bragging about how you would go to Robert's country club and play racquetball together and then have a three-martini lunch. Carlton, I felt you were so enamored with Robert because you had not traveled in the same circles in school, but now that you are a successful banker and could maybe do Robert's business some good, he was happy to wine and dine you. In school Robert was one of the rich, handsome, and bright guys who didn't think they had to play by the rules. You were the class clown and amused everyone with your antics. What you didn't realize was that the popular crowd made fun of you behind your back and would never include you in any of their plans. Don't you see, Carlton, he is still using you."

"Yes, I guess you are right about Robert. I felt like we were back in school, and he had finally accepted me for who I am, but no, he is using me. Won't he be surprised when I turn him down for the business loan he has asked me for? I am going to make sure I am the one to tell him. Oh, Elaine, I am so sorry. I didn't mean to hurt you. Will you please forgive me?"

Elaine sat down and her purple complexion started to return to normal. "Yes, I forgive you. But you must promise me that from now on you will keep private anything that anyone tells you. Promise?"

"Oh, yes I promise."

Elaine and I left Carlton's apartment and went down to have coffee. When we were sitting at the table, I asked her if she wanted to talk about it.

"I guess it isn't that big of a thing now," she said, "But I wanted to kill myself back then. I didn't tell anyone because I was sure they wouldn't believe me. I prayed every night until I got my next period. I was so sure I had become pregnant after the attack. From then on, I avoided Robert and his friends and became a little mouse in the corner. My friends couldn't understand it when I didn't try out for the spring play because I had always had an acting role from the time I was in Junior High. I was passionate about performing, but when I heard that Robert was going to play the male lead, I had to withdraw my application. That attack changed everything in my life until I was in college."

I comforted, "I think you are very brave, Elaine, and you can believe me when I tell you I will never tell a living soul about this. Now, let's go see a funny movie and laugh until our sides hurt."

]

Chapter 27
The Poker Game

One of the funniest things I remember seeing in all of the time I lived at Eden Estates concerned a poker game taking place, late at night, in the community room. I had gone down to fill my plastic jugs with filtered water supplied by the management and was surprised at what I found. I was not the only one to be surprised. As I entered the room several faces looked up and were startled to see me. They almost looked like I caught them with their hands in the cookie jar.

"Hello Betty, what brings you here at this time of night?" one of them said. "We couldn't sleep, so we decided to come down here and keep each other company. We watched TV for a little while but after 10 o'clock there isn't much on. Caroline asked if we had ever played poker, and we all said we had played when we were much younger so we decided that poker would be more fun than TV." Ruth was twisting her hands in a nervous gesture and the others looked like they wished to be anywhere but where they were.

I saw four women gathered to play an all-American brand of poker, and it was clear they didn't want to be disturbed. Frankly, I was surprised at who I found around the table strewn with poker chips and playing cards. These individuals didn't normally associate with each other on any regular basis. Between them they had varying degrees of health, wealth, education, and backgrounds. Other than living in the same building, there wasn't anything I could think of to draw them together. At least, that is what I had thought before I witnessed this scene. Evidently, they had more in common than anyone knew.

First there was Caroline, a small bird-like woman who seldom was the big loser. With her sidewise glances, it looked like she was spying on the others, not entirely engaged with the group and she had a nervous habit of running her fingers through her thick white hair. To say she was a proper lady would be an understatement. Her clothes were not always the most fashionable, but they were exquisitely tailored and fit her like a glove. You wouldn't catch Caroline in a T-shirt and jeans even if she was on the way to the car wash. Her hair and makeup were understated and appropriate for whatever circumstances were presented. That is why I was surprised to see her in this setting.

Then there was Ruth. Now she was exactly the type who would enjoy this type of activity I remember thinking. She was an imposing figure around the building, being almost six feet tall and big boned, Ruth did occasionally push her weight around if it fit her purposes. Not many people argued with Ruth, not even Marianne. Her monthly trip to one of the casinos in the area was no secret. On the third of each month her social security check arrived. She would walk away from the mail boxes, climb into her car, and drive to her bank where she would remove enough cash to see her through the day. Then she was on to a casino. Ruth told us many times that she enjoyed playing the slot machines or spending time in the poker parlor. Ruth loved gambling in any form, but she never shared the results of her adventures. We never knew if she had won a large pot or came home broke, and certainly everyone knew better than to inquire.

I was even more alarmed at seeing the next person that was around the table. My friend, Elaine didn't look at me, but her face was a bright shade of red, even to the tips of her ears.

"Elaine," I said, "I am surprised to find you here."

Elaine replied, "We're just having a friendly game of poker. I don't have to only hang around with you all of the time. I can see whoever I want to." I didn't press her further.

Other than the short conversations I had with two people at the table, I knew they were all hoping I would collect my water and exit the room quickly, and that is exactly what I did. While I was collecting my water, I could hear whispers across the room and a few snickers. As I left the room, I tried to ignore what I saw on the floor. Evidently, the game had been going on for a while because the pile of clothing strewn around the table, beside each of their chairs, had grown to more than a few pieces. I could tell just by looking at the piles who had been winning and who was losing.

Ruth was almost fully dressed, but poor Caroline was looking cold, due to the fact that she was only wearing her underwear at this point.

Thinking about when I first walked into the room and viewed what was on the table, something bothered me. I saw poker chips and a deck of cards, but no money was present. Evidently these women enjoyed playing strip poker instead of the more traditional variety. I never was able to get those images out of my mind. When I recalled it now, I still had to chuckle.

Chapter 28
The Detecting Begins

The residents were told that Detective Lindley and his partner, Detective Scott were going to come to Eden Estates the next day and do some more investigating. Everyone was requested to make themselves available and to tell them the absolute truth. Linda made it clear if anyone held anything back or lied to the police, there would be severe consequences that could even result in their arrest for impeding a police investigation. Most of the people seemed to have no trouble with that, but I am sure some of them were wetting their Depends.

After the notices had come out about the police returning to our building, several people congregated in the community room to share what they thought would happen when the police came.

Alice seemed to be extremely nervous for some reason. She was actually trembling. "What if they ask me where I was when Betty was killed? I was home in bed but nobody can vouch for me."

Several of the residents voiced the same concern. How were they going to prove they had no part in my death? I hoped the next few days were going to really narrow down the suspect pool. I couldn't wait.

I saw the detectives sitting in their car in the parking lot of Eden Estates, and by listening in on their conversation, I learned a lot about the two people who were going to put everyone who lived here through hell until my murderer was apprehended.

It became apparent by their conversation that Detective David Lindley was new to the homicide unit. Even though he had spent 24 years in other departments in the Margin police department, this was a new experience for him. He told Detective Scott. "I didn't really think about becoming a homicide detective, but when the chief approached me about this position, I was feeling burned out on the vice squad, so I took a leap of faith and here I am." I thought he looked considerably older than he probably was — thinning brownish-gray hair, padded love handles around his middle, chewed fingernails, and steely brown eyes that probably held secrets about things he had seen and heard in all of his years on the force.

Even though Detective Sandra Scott was much younger than her partner, she knew she was more experienced in the aspects of homicidal detection. "I know we haven't worked together very long, but I believe if we bring all of our individual experiences to this case, we will be successful in finding the guilty party."

Detective Scott talked a good game, but her actions and body language sent a different message. She absentmindedly ran her right hand through her short blond hair, pulled on her earring, and adjusted her glasses. I knew that nervous habits were done subconsciously when people don't want to admit they are frightened about something they fear may happen. I wondered what she was feeling about this case, and I was having a hard time tuning into her thoughts. That can happen when a person is skilled in hiding their feelings, and I hoped Detective Scott would let down her guard so I could figure out what I needed to tell her so she and Detective Lindley would be successful. It was extremely important to me that these detectives solve this case.

Detective Scott said, "I think we should start out with everyone in the community room and watch the reactions of the residents when we tell them we will be separating them for the major part of the investigation. Some of them will get very nervous about us entering their homes to question them and that could work to our advantage."

"I think that's a good plan," Detective Lindley agreed. "While you are speaking to them, I will be trying to notice any overt nervousness, suspicious glances between people, or anyone who says they do not want us going into their apartments."

Detective Lindley paused before he said, "Before we go in, I want to ask you a personal question, is that OK?"

"Certainly," she said.

"Well, when I first came into the department and the other detectives heard you would be my new partner, they started to snicker and give me pats on the back. When I asked Detective Larson about their reaction, he told me you had been known to have a special gift that can sometimes lead you to answers no one else had been able to obtain. He said you had the ability to 'read' people, even dead ones, and that you could also see something called an aura surrounding living people. Is this true?"

Detective Scott looked at him as she was exiting their vehicle and said, "Don't believe everything you hear, Detective."

The detectives entered the building and were happy to see the entire community room was filled with most, if not all, of the residence.

"I know we were here just yesterday, but this is an ongoing investigation into the death of Betty Nelson, and I would appreciate your cooperation. My team and I will be meeting with each of you and continue taking statements from you concerning this matter. You can all go back to your apartments now, and we will be with you shortly. Please remain in your homes until you have been interviewed by myself or Detective Scott. Your honesty and feelings about this situation will be appreciated."

I followed the detectives around the building and tried to listen in on many of the interviews. Because I could float from room to room, I could listen in on two conversations at the same time if the two detectives were in two different apartments that shared a wall, I could hear all the people speaking at the same time. I was more interested in listening to the people that I didn't get along with than the ones who were my friends.

The detectives were very methodical about how they would conduct the interviews. They started on the fourth floor and worked their way down to the first floor. Since they had not spent much time with any of the residents, Detective Lindley had no preconceived ideas about who did or didn't get along with the victim (me).

The interviews took most of the day and many people were getting more anxious as the hours went by and they waited, not knowing what anyone else had been telling the police. It did not make the wait any easier. Many of the people were trying to remember what had happened that awful morning. What if they couldn't recollect all the facts with the commotion that was taking place on first floor? Would the police think they were lying because their stories did not match exactly what someone else had told them? They were all thinking, "Oh, this is so nerve wracking. I wish they would get to me soon."

Floating around the building I saw Detective Scott knocking on Marianne's door, and I wanted to sit in on this interview. I couldn't wait to hear what Marianne would tell the detective. Would she come right out and confess to killing me? Would she lie about how she had treated me or just put on her snide smile and act like she had nothing to do with the tension that existed in the building? I couldn't wait to see what Marianne would say. I was almost giddy.

Marianne lived on the second floor, so she had lots of time to think of what she was going to tell the detective. When the knock came, she jumped like an electrical charge had gone through her body. She opened the door to Detective Scott, one of the team of investigators she had seen that morning.

"Marianne Taylor? May I come in? I am Detective Scott, and I would like to ask you some questions."

"Of course, Detective, have a seat. Would you like a cup of coffee or tea, or a glass of water?'

"No, thank you Mrs. Taylor. I would just like to sit and talk to you for a few minutes." Detective Scott took a small notebook out of her pocket and settled down in a huge recliner in Marianne's living room. The apartments were very small so no matter where Marianne sat she was never farther away than six feet from Detective Scott. It made for a very cozy arrangement.

"Mrs. Taylor, when was the last time you remember seeing Mrs. Nelson?"

"I probably saw her on Saturday at the mailboxes about 1:00. She was visiting with a couple of people. I don't remember who they were exactly, but I know it wasn't Carol or Maureen because Betty didn't speak to them. Oh, now I remember. Betty was talking to Tootsie and JoAnn. Betty liked them a lot. They hung out together and went shopping all of the time. They all sat at the same table in the community room and many times they shared a pizza or something one of them had cooked for dinner. Betty was always trying to get people to be more active, but old people are set in their ways, and we don't like change. She did her laundry any time she wanted and said she would park anywhere she wanted even though I told her repeatedly that she couldn't. Betty didn't understand there are rules here that we have followed for many years, and I have always felt she just didn't fit in."

Detective Scott was very interested in the diatribe that Marianne had offered, even though she had only been asked when was the last time she had seen me. She made several entries in her notebook, and I saw that she had written, "Gave too much information. Why is Mrs. Taylor offering so much information? What is she trying to hide?"

"Yes, I have heard that you and she didn't see eye-to-eye on many levels. I assume you were alone about midnight on Monday morning the eighth of November?"

"Of course, I was alone. I was asleep."

"Did you hear anything that woke you up at any time that night?"

"No, I only got up about 4:00 to go to the bathroom, but that happens every night. I have a weak bladder, you know."

"So, you are saying that you were asleep, alone in your apartment from what time Sunday night?"

"I came upstairs about 7:00 pm because I wanted to watch the football game and have something to eat. I always sit in front of the TV and eat supper when the game is on. Anyone can tell you that. They know I am a great fan of the Green Bay Packers and never miss a game. Some of the others watch the game together on the big screen TV in the community room, but I don't like most of those people, so I watch it alone in my apartment. I turned in about 11:00 and fell asleep with no trouble."

"I have been told, Mrs. Taylor, that you and the deceased have had harsh words about many issues in the last year. Can you tell me why that is?"

"Betty was a newcomer, and she was friendly to everyone. I felt like she was going to come in here and take over. A lot of us have lived here a long, long time, and we like things done in a certain way. We don't feel like we need to share our laundry time or our parking spaces with anyone. Betty always wanted everything to be equal for everyone. Well, let me tell you, some people are more equal than others. I heard she didn't fit in with the writing group either because she wanted to change the way that worked also. Stella told me that when Betty couldn't get her way, she quit the group. Seems kind of selfish to me. Betty was so nice to everyone until they crossed her, and then she became vicious. I knew nobody could be that sweet all the time. It was just an act to get everyone to like her. I don't care who likes me and who doesn't, and I don't take crap from anyone."

"That sounds almost vindictive Mrs. Taylor. Do you know of anyone else who felt this way about Mrs. Nelson?"

"Well, Maureen and Carol certainly did. They called her, Mrs. Do-Goody."

"It sounds to me like the only people who felt that way were people who Mrs. Nelson stood up to and that everyone else liked her and wanted to spend time with her."

"Well, I never," said Marianne. "Are you saying that one of us three killed Betty and there was no one else who had a reason to hate her?"

"I am just saying that everyone else liked Mrs. Nelson, so I need to look very carefully at the people who didn't." Detective Scott only had one more question for Marianne. "Can you think of anyone who would want to see Mrs. Nelson dead?"

"Well, even though my friends and I didn't like Betty, we wouldn't do anything like that to her. Did we do everything we could so that she would want to move out? Yes, we did. But to actually kill her? It gives me the creeps because we don't know who did it, so we don't know who we can trust and who we can't. I'm thinking of buying a gun to protect myself. Right now, all I have is a baseball bat behind my bedroom door. Betty was disgustingly sweet and thoughtful, so if she wasn't safe, who is?"

"I don't think buying a gun is the answer, Mrs. Taylor," Detective Scott said. "Unless you take extensive gun training, it can be very dangerous having a handgun around." Detective Scott got up to leave. "Well, thank you for your time. If I need any more information from you, I will be back. Goodbye, Mrs. Taylor, and please don't make any plans to leave the state."

When Detective Scott left Marianne's apartment, she took a break on the patio and went over in her mind what to do next. Sometimes this gift of hers was not very helpful, but this time it spoke volumes. Being able to see or feel other people's auras told her much more than their words could ever reveal. Take this last suspect she had talked with. Marianne started with a mostly orange aura meaning she had strong opinions and was not afraid to use them to control others. She gave people pause because she could be manipulative, hot headed, and quick tempered. But the most disturbing color surrounding Marianne was brown, given to negative thoughts and feelings that could have an effect on anyone within five feet of her. She gave off the bad vibe you hear people talk about, and it explained why Marianne had trouble getting along with others who came too close to her. This also told Detective Scott that Marianne could be untruthful in order to make herself appear more caring and thoughtful, which she wasn't.

Because Detective Scott also had the ability to not only read people's auras but could also communicate with the dead, she was often brought in on cases where there were multiple suspects. In many cases, the victim chose to hang around where they had been killed. She hadn't seen or heard from Mrs. Nelson, but she could still sense her presence. She had to find a way to communicate with Betty Nelson because there had been several instances where the victims themselves helped to solve the case.

Well, watching Detective Scott talk to Marianne didn't tell me anything I didn't already know. How disappointing! I was almost sure it was Marianne and that the police would get her to confess, unless of course, she lied to the detective. I was hoping as time went on that Marianne would let something slip that would prove she killed me, but for now I needed to move on.

I don't know why I believed this but I did feel like Detective Scott could tell I was around during the questioning, and I needed a way to communicate with her if I was going to help her in her quest for my killer. I hadn't tried to communicate with anyone since I died, but I knew there had to be a way, and all I needed to do was to find it.

I knew I couldn't touch her because I didn't know how it would affect her, although if she really had a special gift, maybe she would be the only one who could feel me. I could try that and see what happened. Or, I could try to speak to her telepathically. I wondered if she was the type of person who would be able to get messages that moved through her mind, and she would listen and try to figure out what they meant. I was going to find Detective Scott and try these new ideas. It was going to be very frustrating if she had these special gifts of perception, but I had no way to communicate with her.

I found her walking down the hall to Carol's apartment and followed her. She sat down on one of the benches along the wall and was entering notes into a notebook. At first, she didn't seem to notice me or know that I was there. I sat down next to her, and she stopped writing in her book. She looked up and down the hall like she expected someone to be there. I touched her, and she was startled getting goosebumps on her arms. Oh boy, she was aware of me, she knew I was there, but I don't know how she was going to interpret what she was feeling. I touched her again and this time she just smiled.

"Mrs. Nelson, is that you?"

I shouted, "Yes, it's me. It's me, it's me."

"I thought it was you. You have been following me around, haven't you?"

"Yes, I have been watching you and Detective Lindley and the residents here ever since…… ever since it happened. I want to help you discover who did this to me. I want to see them punished."

It became clear to both of us at the same time what would happen if anyone came down the hall and heard Detective Scott seemingly talking to herself. She would look like a crazy person and probably be taken off this case.

I said, "Maybe we should not communicate in public places from now on. Can you read my thoughts without me speaking?"

"Yes, I can. That would be the preferred method for us to speak to each other. I would like you to accompany me when I interview everyone because you would know who was lying or who was being truthful. Then I will go somewhere out of earshot of anyone else, and we can compare notes. By the way, I think we should speak later. I want to ask you what you thought of the interview I just did with Marianne."

I decided to follow Detective Scott when she interviewed some of the other residence. Maybe, now that I shared a secret with one of the investigators, I could relax a little and let her do her job. I was beginning to think that we might really find out what had happened to me and why. I was not in this alone anymore. I had someone I could trust and communicate with.

As Detective Scott next went to the second floor to interview Carol, I thought back to another time I had started out with a good idea to get everyone involved in doing something for the betterment of all and ended up in another fracas.

Chapter 29
Still wondering….

I was beginning to think I was not considering all of the circumstances of my life that could have led to this outcome. Maybe someone from my past was responsible, and I just hadn't wanted to look at that possibility. I am sure there were times where I could have been more understanding even with my friends let alone the people who made me angry.

Maybe there was someone from Iowa that had come up to Margin and found a way into the apartment building. I missed several of the people in Anthony Falls and had not maintained a close relationship with all my friends there. I was so concerned with making friends and building a life here that I didn't give much thought to people I had known for forty years. How selfish of me.

We had many good times going out together, taking classes, even helping each other raise our children. Most of us went to the same church and belonged to the same clubs and community groups. So we knew each other very well. A few of my old friends had called me and asked about my "new life" but I never invited them to come visit me even though I missed them. When had I become so shallow, so unconcerned about others? With how I had been treating my old friends, I was beginning to think what happened to me could just as well have happened a long time ago while I was still living in Iowa. "Think, Betty, think," I was telling myself. I needed to remember activities where something wasn't right, where something happened that might explain why I was dead.

Chapter 30
The Imposter

I was trying to recollect everyone who lived in the building and determine if they were a danger to me. There were a few people I was going to give a lot of consideration to because they were not the ones who called attention to themselves or made trouble. So they had fallen through the cracks in my thought process.

If there was one thing that leveled the playing field for everyone in the building, it was the fact that nobody could afford to live in a market value apartment. We were people, for many reasons, marginalized as low-income citizens. Most of the residence found themselves in a precarious financial situation through no fault of their own. Life happens.

One woman fled a dangerously abusive relationship with very little of her belongings that she had accumulated throughout her lifetime. She started over when she was past middle age, a situation I had been lucky enough to avoid. Andrea worked full time and also spent a lot of time with her family. Occasionally, I would see her at the mailboxes or in the parking lot when she was coming or going with her many activities. I don't know if I had ever really had a conversation with Andrea. I wouldn't be able to describe her personality. I just knew she was the youngest tenant in the building and dressed in the latest fashions. I was aware that some of the older residents were jealous of her figure and her ability to take part in many of the things they had enjoyed in their "past lives", as they referred to their younger years.

I couldn't identify with all the residents who lived through extremely dangerous situations. I found that some of these women became hoarders, and after hearing their story, I could almost understand their thinking. If I had lost everything from my past life, I might also feel the need to hold on tenaciously to what I had acquired in my new life. But, I still felt sorry for them. Hoarding is a mental illness that I hoped I would never fall to.

My story was different than many others because most of my money was used to pay my late husband's hospital bills when our Medicare and other medical insurance ran out. I had lived a solid middle-class lifestyle, so finding myself in a position where the funds my husband and I invested for our retirement years were greatly depleted was scary and worrisome to me. Luckily, my children stepped up and found me a clean, well-managed, affordable solution to my housing issue, and I had loved living at Eden Estates.

Now, we come to Laura Lawrence. Laura moved into Eden Estates a year before I did. She lived on the third floor and enjoyed the advantage of living in the nicest corner apartment in the building. Laura would come down to the community room frequently, and she had a great sense of humor so she was fun to take a coffee break with. I remember one day Laura entered the community room in a flurry wearing a flowing caftan with a cloud of Chanel # 5 surrounding her. Her flaming red hair and long artificial nails made her stand out in a place where jeans and T-shirts were the normal attire you would see in the community room. I could never say that Laura was a shy or retiring person, but I was always a little surprised when she seemed to use up all of the oxygen in the room as soon as she crossed the threshold. She never cared who was speaking or what topic was being discussed because once she was present, it was all about her.

"I can't believe my good fortune. My son and his family are taking me on a Disney cruise next February. Oh my, oh my, I was so surprised when Bob called and asked if I would be interested in joining them on their winter vacation. Can you imagine, spending a week with my grandchildren enjoying the warm weather and being entertained every day by their favorite princesses and other Disney characters? It is amazing the same things that added so much to my childhood are the same things my grandchildren are enjoying now. It's a common connection we can all enjoy."

Tootsie said, "That is wonderful. Your children are so nice to you; they often come visit you and take you out to dinner and to movies. I wish some other children would be more attentive to their parents who live here. I know there are residents here who have their children live close by, but those children never call or visit. That is so sad. I am also lucky because my kids take good care of me."

Laura added, "This will be the second cruise they are going to take me on. The first one was a Caribbean cruise to San Juan, Puerto Rico, St Croix, and St Maarten. And yes, I do appreciate all that my children do for me."

I remember asking, "Didn't your children buy you a new phone a few months ago?"

"Well, yes they did, but I didn't ask them to," Laura replied in a voice that seemed almost apologetic.

JoAnn looked over at Laura and asked, "And didn't you tell us that that Bob bought you a new laptop last Christmas?"

"I didn't ask for that either. My old one had just died, and Bob knows I need a computer. I am investigating our genealogy and building a family tree so that our children and grandchildren will know their history."

Carlton had just joined the group and had heard the last ten minutes of the conversation. "Last year you were very happy with the new 50 inch TV your son bought you. Do your kids always buy you everything you want?"

"No, of course not. They just want my life to be as pleasant as possible. Can I help it if my children earn good money and want to share it? They also give generously to their church and favorite charities. I guess I raised very thoughtful children, and I am thankful to them both."

Marianne had been sitting with her posse listening to all of this and said, "It sounds like you are their favorite charity."

We all laughed, but I think a lot of people were jealous that Laura's kids were so good to her.

Later on, when I saw Laura in the hallway, I told her to just ignore the people who were jealous. I said, "Some people also think I am spoiled because my children help me out whenever they can." I added, "Don't let it get to you. Just be grateful."

The issue was forgotten until after Laura and her family returned from the latest cruise in February. Her son was helping Laura get her luggage up to her apartment, and he stopped into the community room on his way out. We asked him how the vacation went.

"Oh, it was really special seeing my mom interact with my children and all of the Disney characters. We went to a special Princess breakfast where my girls dressed up in their fancy dresses and then all of the different princesses came by the table and talked to them. They also got several autographs. Mom really enjoyed being in the pool with the kids and wandering around the ship. We are so grateful that she took us on this trip, I don't know how we will ever be able to thank her."

I was shocked when Bob said that and commented, "Well, I know all of the wonderful things you buy your mom like her TV, phone, and computer. This will go a long way to thank you."

Bob laughed, "You have got to be kidding. I could never afford to buy all of those expensive things. Mom pays for all of that herself. She paid for our cruises also. Where did you get the idea that I was paying for the vacations? Well, goodnight, it was great seeing all of you again."

When Bob left, we looked at each other and shook our heads. "Well, how do you like those apples? All this time Laura was telling us that Bob was buying things for her, and it was a lie. How can she afford to do all of this spending?" I wondered.

"I don't know, but I'm going to find out," mumbled JoAnn.

The next day JoAnn went into Linda's office and told her what we had found out about Laura. Linda was also shocked and said she would look into the situation.

From then on, Laura barely left her apartment, and when she saw us having coffee as she came down to retrieve her mail, she looked at all of us and said, "Why did you have to put your nose into my business? You could have just made a decision to keep what you found out to yourselves instead of going to Linda. It is none of anyone's business how much money I have. You will all be very sorry for what you have done. Just you wait and see."

A month later there was a very interesting buzz going around the building. It was just gossip, of course, but everyone was talking about it. When the cloud lifted and the facts were verified, it was important information that made many of us angry. JoAnn was in the outer office when Laura was talking to Linda about her real financial situation. She couldn't help but hear what was being said in very loud voices. JoAnn could have left the office and not listened to the voices behind the closed door, but what was the fun in that. When we heard the whole scoop, it was worse than anyone could have imagined.

It seems that when Laura moved into Eden Estates, she hid an enormous amount of her investments from Linda. Evidently, she owned two rental properties that she had in her daughter's name so they would not show up on her financial report. She also had a very large amount of money invested in offshore accounts that would have eliminated her as a candidate for affordable housing.

A week later Laura moved out of the building in the middle of the night, and she was never missed.

CHAPTER 31
JoAnn & Elaine

I thought I would find Detective Lindley and see who he was questioning. It took a while to find him as he had been to several apartments during the day.

I was starting to think it may be inconsequential who murdered me. Why couldn't I just move on to where ever I was supposed to end up? Why did I think I needed to stay around and eavesdrop on this investigation? Why did I think I knew more than anyone else and had the audacity to believe I would be able to solve this mystery more competently than trained law enforcement professionals? It was because I was just as obstinate and controlling dead as I had been when I was alive.

I found Detective Lindley in JoAnn's apartment and even though she was weeping, the things she was telling him did not jive with her emotions. JoAnn almost looked embarrassed when she said, "I know Betty was a really good person and she did a lot for most of us in the building, but she also had a hard time letting anyone else get their way. I feel it is important that people stick up for themselves, but sometimes Betty could be a little abrupt. Many of the people have lived here a long time, and they get kind of stuck in their ways. So when Betty would tell them what to do, they would be hurt and get angry."

"I never told people what to do," I thought. "I just wanted them to play by the rules that were printed in very large letters in the residents' handbook. How dare JoAnn say that! I guess she wasn't a friend of mine after all." I was wondering if the other people I thought would be on my side felt the same way. Maybe I should have paid more attention to my friends than I had thought necessary. Maybe I had gone about this all wrong. Oh no, it couldn't be one of my friends that did this to me, could it?

Since I was invisible I could enter any apartment at any time I wanted to, not just when the police were questioning everyone. This might be fun after all.

I floated into Elaine's apartment and was shocked at what I was witnessing. I heard there were people who did housework in very little clothing, but to find Elaine vacuuming her living room in a state of complete undress was alarming. Since she had already been interviewed, she felt confident neither of the detectives would be knocking on her door again today. She was whistling and pushing the vacuum around without a care in the world. I was thinking she didn't look to bad for being 73 years old, but now I knew for sure Elaine colored her hair because there was gray hair everywhere on her body except her head. Oh, who cares who does what to make themselves look better? Certainly, not me.

When Elaine finished vacuuming, she put the vacuum away in the walk-in closet in the hallway. She then went to her bedroom and stepped up to a beautiful, solid oak file cabinet where she started to file a pile of documents. It had to take a long time to accumulate that many papers, so I guessed this was not a task Elaine performed on a regular basis. She only worked on the filing for about twenty minutes and then gathered the items she would need to scrub her floor leaving the filing unfinished.

I became bored watching her do housework until Elaine's phone rang, and she took a break in her task list to answer the call. "Hello," Elaine answered cheerfully. "Oh, hi JoAnn. What are you doing?" Because JoAnn and Elaine lived next door to each other, I could watch both at the same time and monitor this phone call.

"I am scared to death Elaine," JoAnn said with fear dripping from every word. "What if I say something to the police that makes them think I killed Betty? I get really nervous talking to the police and can get really mixed up sometimes."

"JoAnn, just tell them the truth, and you won't have anything to worry about." Elaine assured her. "We were all asleep when Betty was murdered, and that is why we were all so shocked the next morning when Betty's body was found. What do you suppose the police think us we seniors do in the middle of the night? Have wild parties and push each other up and down the hallways in grocery carts? No, they think we are doing exactly what anyone else would be doing, sleeping. That is why I think this mystery is going to be hard to solve. Everyone knows we are all asleep in the middle of the night, so it wouldn't be very hard to walk around the building unnoticed. It still gives me the creeps to think that someone who lives here is that evil."

As I moved from apartment to apartment, I viewed people going about their business. Later, I noticed that Elaine and JoAnn were in Elaine's apartment, and they were discussing what to do about the police. Elaine asked JoAnn, "How much should we be telling the police? Do you think we should offer information they haven't asked for or just answer their questions?"

"What do you mean, Elaine? What else can we tell them?"

"Just think of all the times we were in the community room and someone made us all uncomfortable with their bossy ways. If we repeated some of the things people talked about, it could get a lot of people in trouble."

"Elaine," JoAnn remarked. "We need to tell them anything we can think of because they won't know all of the right questions to ask us if we don't tell them what we know. They don't know what goes on around here, so they may miss some information that could help them find the guilty party."

"I guess you are right JoAnn. But what I am talking about are instances where the cops would not have a clue about certain people or events. People who live here, and people who don't. Like what about the time Betty's family visited, and we could hear them shouting at each other all the way down the hall to the laundry room? What about that, huh? Should we tell them everything we heard that time'?

"Well," said JoAnn. "Yes, we should."

"Can you actually recall what happened that day? I remember bits and pieces, so maybe between the two of us we can sort out what really happened. Are you willing to help me put together a cohesive story that is not too far-fetched? One the detectives will believe?"

"Are you kidding? They wouldn't believe half of what really goes on around here even if we could remember everything. But I think we should try."

"OK, then. Do you remember if it was only Robert and Sherrie or were Susan and Anthony there too that day?"

"I think it was her whole family. They had come to celebrate someone's birthday, but I don't remember whose it was."

"You are right, that is where it all began. Her son was saying it would have been nice if they could have gone to his house for the party because the space was bigger and they could go outside on the patio to play bocce ball in the backyard."

"That is when his sister, Susan, started yelling about how come they always went to his house for family get-togethers because her house was just as nice and it wasn't much further away than his house."

JoAnn said, "Then Betty's daughter-in-law, Sherrie, said their home and yard were indeed larger than his sister's and closer to Betty, so it only made sense they would go to their house. Betty spoke up and said that no one ever came to visit her like they said they would when they convinced her to move to Wisconsin from Iowa after their dad died. Betty said, 'You told me I would see you all often. You said you would show me around and how to find things I would need like the grocery store and church. I had never driven here because your dad always did the driving when we went anywhere. How was I supposed to know once you got me here you would abandon me and let me get lost driving round trying to find things? I don't even know how to get to either of your houses from here because you have never let me drive there by myself. Robert, when you invited me to Amber's school concert, I made up an excuse that I had other plans because I knew none of you would have time to come get me. I was afraid I would get lost and disappoint Amber if I said I would be there and then wasn't'."

Elaine said, "Then all went quiet. I remember we had to get a lot closer to Betty's door to hear the rest of the conversation."

JoAnn said she would never forget the next things that were said by Susan. "OK, so you have a bigger, fancier property but at least Anthony is home every night instead of gallivanting all over the country schmoozing with bigwigs just so you can make more money than God. Maybe if you were home more, you would notice your lovely wife has taken up tennis at the fancy-schmancy country club you are always bragging about. I have heard some of those lessons are very private and last longer than normal. Some of them even take place in the club swimming pool."

"Well, I never," Sherrie shouted. "You take that back. The tennis pro suggested we spend some time loosening up in the pool before my lesson, that's all."

"Oh, is that what they are calling it now? Loosening up?"

"Just shut up, Susan," Robert said. "What my wife and I do in our spare time is none of your business. And I suppose you and your uneducated husband like living paycheck to paycheck so you can stay home and watch TV and eat bon-bons all day. You know you never paid your share when mom moved here, so maybe I will just send you a bill for your half."

"Susan's husband, Anthony, then thought it was time to put in his two cents worth. 'Let's just cool down everybody. Can't you see how upset Betty is right now? We all came to see her and to celebrate a birthday. So let's just back off and spend our time with Betty.'"

JoAnn remembered, "That is when it got all quiet, and we had to get right next to Betty's door in order to hear anything."

"How much longer was it when they started up again?" asked Elaine.

"About three or four minutes. I remember we were getting bored, and we were going to leave, and then we heard Betty saying, 'Well, I think enough has been said today, and to say I am disappointed is an understatement. I thought I had raised two loving and caring children who would do anything for each other and me if things got tough. But, now I know differently. You are all out for yourselves no matter the cost. You are willing to drag each other through the mud and say unkind things just to build your own egos. I guess I will not be seeing you all together anymore because I will not put myself through this again. I don't have any idea if any of this is even true, or that it is any of my business anyway.'"

"Oh sure, Mom, you always believe your precious son and his cold-as-fish-wife," Susan spewed through clenched teeth. "Anthony and I do as much as we can for you, and you know that. I know we don't come see you as often as we should, but I promise, that is going to change. Please forgive me for the things I have said today. I think it is time for us to leave. Come on kids, get your shoes on, give nana a hug, and let's get out of here."

JoAnn grimaced, "I was so sure we were going to get caught with our ears to Betty's door, but we got to the stairwell just in time to miss the family making a mass exodus. I wanted to go back and ask Betty if she was OK, but then she would know we had heard the whole thing. It was really hard for the next few days to see Betty in the hallway and not say something. Betty never said anything to me about it, so she was probably embarrassed to reveal the skeletons in her closet. I felt bad for her."

Chapter 32
The Truth Comes Out

I was so happy I began remembering more and more about my death — how it happened, who did it and why. I know I can't dream like people who are still breathing but thoughts were coming to me faster than I could process them. For some reason I felt that Nick Olson had a hand in my demise. I couldn't really remember exactly what had happened, but the memories were returning. After a few minutes the entire episode flashed before my eyes, and I could hardly believe what I was seeing. I started to shake when the truth was reveled but I knew I couldn't keep this to myself.

I was determined to get this message to Detective Scott as soon as I could. I heard Linda saying the police were coming back the next Monday to continue their investigation. Because time had no meaning for me, I didn't care it might be a while until I saw Detective Scott again. It seemed like I had just blinked when the detectives were back in the building. They both had taken a list of the people at Eden Estates they wanted to talk to, dividing up the rest of the suspects among themselves. Detective Lindley started where he had left off on the second floor to continue with his investigation. Detective Scott was going to concentrate on the first floor where no one had been questioned yet.

"Let's see if we can finish the first round of questioning today and then get together to eliminate the suspects we both feel have no reason to kill Mrs. Nelson," suggested Detective Lindley.

"Sounds good to me," answered Detective Scott. I started following her as she went down to the end of the hall. Before I said anything to her, I wanted to hear what was said about me in the apartments. Since Marianne didn't live on the first floor, I doubted very much anyone would be making a confession any time soon.

When Detective Scott knocked on the end door there was a very quiet, squeaky voice that called out, "Who's there?"

"This is Detective Scott from the police department. Could you please open the door so we could speak face to face?"

"Well, how can I be sure you are with the police?"

"I can put my badge up by the peep hole, and you can read it if you would like. Here it is. Can you see it?"

"Not actually," the small voice said. "You see I am partially blind so I don't trust that I will be able to read it."

Detective Scott said, "Mrs. Fugtree, I will go next door and get your neighbor, Mrs. Winston. Then she can read my badge and tell you who I am. Is that all right with you? Would you be happy with that?"

"Yes, yes, yes, that would be very helpful."

Detective Scott went across the hall to Mrs. Winston's door and repeated the process of knocking and identifying herself.

Mrs. Winston answered promptly and recognized the detective. "Oh, I was wondering if you would get around to me today. Come in, come in."

"Actually, Mrs. Winston, I would like your help. Mrs Fugtree is having a hard time identifying me, so she really isn't comfortable opening her door. Do you think you could help me gain entry to Mrs. Fugtree's apartment?"

"Oh, sure. Edna Fugtree is afraid of her own shadow. She is in her late nineties and suspects everyone wants to rob her, but I think I can talk her into letting you in." Mrs. Winston went to the door across the hallway and knocked very loud. "Edna, this is Mary-Elizabeth across the hall. There is a very nice detective out here who would like to ask you some questions. She is thinking you may have some answers for her about the terrible thing that happened to Mrs. Nelson a few days ago. Could you open the door dear and let her in?"

Well, playing to Mrs. Fugtree's ego and letting her believe she could help the police solve this case was all it took to encourage her to open the door. The door opened very slowly, and even though it was morning, the inside of Mrs. Fugtree's apartment looked like it could have been midnight.

"Hello, Mrs.Fugtree, and thank you for seeing me. I just want a few minutes of your time, and then you can get back to doing whatever you normally do at this time of day. Would you mind if I sat down?"

"No, that is fine. Would you like some coffee or tea? I was taught to always ask guests if they would like a refreshment when they are in my home."

"I am just fine, thank you."

Detective Scott was wearing a lightweight suit and flat shoes, which is normally a very comfortable ensemble for work. However, it had to be 95 degrees in the apartment, and Mrs. Fugtree was wearing two sweaters, a long skirt, heavy wool socks, and she still looked cold. She was a delicate woman who couldn't have weighed 90 pounds, but because of the clothes she was wearing, it was hard to tell. She could have weighed even less. With most of her hair being meager at best and because she wore it long, she looked like a witch from a long ago fairy tale.

Detective Scott looked around the apartment as she would any unfamiliar place. It was a habit to give anywhere new a once over with her eyes because there were always clues to a person's personality in their home. There were many large, overstuffed furniture pieces that would be right at home in the 1920's or '30's. These apartments were small to begin with, so all of this huge furniture made it seem all the more confined. Mrs. Fugtree had two china cabinets in the living room filled to overflowing with knick-knacks that looked like they had come from the 19th century, and indeed, they might have. Detective Scott knew this was going to be an abbreviated interview because she needed to escape this stifling apartment.

"Mrs. Fugtree, when was the last time you saw Mrs. Nelson?"

Mrs. Fugtree furrowed her brow in concentration and said, "I don't believe I know anyone by that name. No, I am sure I have never met Mrs. Nelson."

"But you have heard that she was found dead didn't you?'

"Oh yes. My neighbors called and told me she was discovered in the trash bin. I couldn't believe that something like that could happen here. Although, since I didn't know her, I just put it out of my mind. Why should I worry about someone I never knew? That doesn't make sense."

Detective Scott already surmised that there was nothing more to learn here, so she thanked Mrs. Fugtree and made a quick exit.

Chapter 33
What is Happening?

It was Monday morning when the detectives returned to Eden Estates to continue their investigation. I was trying to find a time when Detective Scott was between interviews so I could talk to her. After she had interviewed several people on the first floor, she had an unsatisfied look on her face. So she took a cup of coffee out to the patio where she would be the only one enjoying the nice weather. Now was my chance. I floated up next to her and tried to get her attention. I had heard she and Detective Lindley say they would get together when they were finished with the interviews and compare notes. I wanted to communicate with her before anyone else came out here.

I sidled right up close to her and said, "Pssssst, pssst." Detective Scott looked around like she was expecting to see a fly or mosquito. Again, I said, "Pssst, psssst. It's me, Betty."

At that she nodded her head so I would know she could hear me. "Oh, it's you. Have you been watching me interview people? I can't believe some of them are cognizant enough to live on their own. One guy fell asleep in his chair while I was asking him questions."

"Oh, that was Walter Cummings. He isn't the most lively person, but he is such a sweetheart that nobody cares he takes naps during a potluck dinner or in the middle of a conversation."

"Well, did you have anything to add to this investigation?" Detective Scott asked me.

"Actually, I have a lot of important information. I know who killed me."

"Really? Do you also have proof that we could use to take to the DA and get an indictment?"

"I think I might."

By the look on Detective Lindley's face when he entered the patio, it was clear he had not made as much progress when he questioned the residents as he had expected. I had stayed to listen in on the conversation and was not surprised at his lack of success.

"Either everyone in this place has dementia or they are all lying," Detective Lindley complained.

Detective Scott agreed with him. "I don't think anybody wants to tell us what they know because they are afraid to become involved in this investigation. Only a few people had anything negative to say about anyone else. Nobody heard or saw anything out of the ordinary. They swear they only discovered there had been a murder when they saw all of the commotion in the morning."

Detective Lindley said he was going to go interview Linda again, and Detective Scott waited for him to leave so she could continue her conversation with me. "Did you hear all of that Betty?"

"Yes, I did. I can't believe my friends would not tell him the way things really were around here. They saw Marianne and her friends bully someone almost every day. Well, let me tell you what I found out," I said. "I have been trying very hard to remember that day, and I finally did. Do you remember meeting Nick, the maintenance man?" I asked Detective Scott.

"Yes, I think so. Was he the one trying to get the crowd away from the trash room?"

"Yes, that's him. Well, he is Marianne's brother. I offered him a piece of apple pie and coffee last Sunday night. He was here getting an apartment ready for a person who was going to move in here on Monday. After he took his break with me, he went back to work. I was going to start clearing up the dishes when I started feeling ill. So, I went to lay down on the sofa. It was obvious that I never got up. Later that night, he came back into my apartment pushing a grocery cart, and Marianne was with him! Marianne picked up the cups and plates to put them in the sink where she rinsed them out. She then took the coffee creamer and put it back into the refrigerator. Nick was so busy examining my body he didn't even notice what Marianne was doing. All of a sudden, Marianne said, 'Phew, what is that smell?'"

I continued to repeat the conversation and happenings I remembered from that evening.

"I don't know," answered Nick. "But I think it is coming from the body. Oh, God, she is all wet." Marianne came closer to my body and told Nick that the smell was familiar, and definitely, gross. "I think it is pee and crap."

"Is that what happens when we croak?" he answered her.

"I don't know, but I'm not touching her," Marianne replied.

"What do you mean you are not touching her? How do you think we are going to get her into the cart?" Nick asked.

"Well, we better wrap her in something before we move her." Marianne agreed to go get a towel to put under my body. That done, they started to lift me into the grocery cart but my skirt slid up around my waist and my underwear was not doing a very good job of containing the excrement. They struggled to put me into the cart because my back was arched and my arms and legs were stiffly sticking out at unnatural angles. Being shoved headfirst down in the cart with my legs jutting out the top seemed wholly impractical but it must have been the only way they could get me to fit. My legs kept hitting the edge of the bedroom door, and I cringed every time this happened even though I couldn't feel anything because I could just imagine how it would have hurt.

Marianne said, "Nick, we need to clean up the mess on the sofa before we leave here. I'll see what she has in her closet. Oh, good I found some oxygenated spray that works really well on stains like this. Go ahead, clean it up," Marianne said and handed the spray bottle to Nick.

"Oh no you don't, I'm not cleanin' up that mess. You do it," Nick handed the bottle back.

"Oh hell, you sissy, then I'll do it." Marianne liberally sprayed the sofa and then used some towels to scrub the mess. She then put the soiled towels on top of my body so they could dispose of them at the same time. Nick opened the apartment door slowly and looked up and down the hall. Not seeing anyone he said, "OK, it looks good." When they tried to get the cart out of the apartment, they had to finagle a way to make me go through the doorway with my arms and legs going every which way. They were also concerned that they needed to do this without making too much noise. They carefully rolled the cart down the hall. Marianne went ahead to look around the corner for any unexpected residents because sometimes there were people in the sitting room by the elevator, even late at the night. Nick tried to push the cart into the trash room while Marianne held the heavy door open, but again they had problems with my feet catching on the door jam. They both looked at me and the size of the trash chute door and then at my unshapely form. Nick looked angry and said, "Oh damn, she ain't gonna fit through this here door. I didn't know her body would be so, so hard."

Marianne laughed and said, "Why do you think they call dead bodies a stiff?"

"Be quiet," Nick hissed. He did not think this was a bit funny, and he snarled at her in a softer voice, "We have to take her down in the elevator instead. Come on, Marianne, open the door and check the hallway." Marianne did as she was told moving along the hallway on the way to the elevator. The coast was clear so she pushed the "down" button, the door opened, and the cart was loaded into the elevator. Nick was unhappy that it seemed to be taking so long for the elevator to descend to first floor. "For God's sake, it shouldn't take so long. It never takes no time at all during the day." By the look on his face, I could tell he was getting more and more frustrated. When they arrived on the first floor, Marianne again went ahead to check the hallways.

"Come on, come on," she whispered loudly. Once they arrived at the trash room, they again had trouble getting my body through the doorway. I thought they were making entirely too much noise for no one else to notice, but alas, no one came to investigate. It was as quiet as death. Finally, Nick, Marianne, and my body were next to the huge dumpster. "OK, now how are we going to get her in there?" Marianne asked Nick.

"We just have to grab an arm and leg and lift her up and over the side." Nick made this sound like they were dealing with a bag of cotton balls instead of a stiff, weirdly-angled dead weight body. After several tries and about twenty minutes past, and after they dropped parts of my body back into the wire cart time after time, they finally got me near the top ledge of the dumpster. Nick was sweating profusely, and Marianne looked like she was having a heart attack.

Marianne said, "I thought that if we got her up here, we could just push her in, but either her arm catches on the cart or her legs kick me in the face'"

Nick finally crawled into the smelly, filthy dumpster. He grabbed one of my feet and Marianne took hold of an arm. They pushed and pulled until I finally fell into the container. Nick tried to hide my body by putting trash over it, but due to the strange angles of my appendages, he was having problems disguising my presence. When they were finished and thought I was completely hidden, they exited the trash room. They were both sweating and covered in bodily fluids. After they returned the grocery cart to the storage area, Nick left the building, and Marianne went back to her apartment in a cold sweat.

"What do you think about that?" I asked Detective Scott.

The next day, several people were again gathered in the community room. JoAnn said, "I'm being silly I know, but I feel better being around other people right now. I know I am safe in my apartment. Ever since we were told Betty was killed in her own apartment, I just want to be with other people."

"I know what you mean," said Tootsie. "Every time I hear someone in the hallway, I look over at the door and shiver."

Many others in the room agreed with them. I could tell because they were nodding their heads as they listened to JoAnn and Tootsie.

One person who didn't say or do anything was Marianne. Nick entered the community room and looked around. When he spotted Marianne, he nodded his head to the left in an almost imperceptible manner and left the room.

In a few minutes, Marianne slowly rose from her chair and gathered her cell phone, keys, and a magazine, telling her friends she had to make some phone calls and walked out to the hallway. No one even gave her a second look.

I stayed with her in the elevator because I wanted to make sure not to lose track of her. When the doors opened, she flew down the hall to her apartment where Nick was waiting for her. He was pacing back and forth and looked like he would jump out of his skin when she came through the door, almost as if he had been expecting someone else.

"What are you doing here, Nick? We can't be seen together, especially now."

"I know, I know. But when I see people talkin' about what happened and guessing who done it, I get really scared, like they knowed it was me."

"Don't talk crazy, Nick. Nobody is going to think you had anything to do with Betty. Why would they? You didn't treat her any different than you did anyone else. Even me."

"Well, as long as we got rid of the evidence, I guess it'll be OK."

"What evidence, Nick? You never told me how you did it."

"Oh, didn't I? I thought I told you I put the poison in her coffee creamer. But, now that you got rid of it, we don't have nothin' to worry about." When Marianne turned pale and didn't answer Nick back, he looked at her and asked, "You did get rid of it, didn't you?"

"Well, I didn't know the poison was in the creamer, so I just put it back in the fridge in Betty's apartment."

"What did you do with the coffee cups?"

"I put them in the sink with the rest of the dishes."

"Oh, my God, Marianne! They will find the poison in the creamer and know it was me."

"How will they know it was you who put it in there? She has company for coffee in her apartment all of the time. I have seen lots of her friends go in there."

"Yes, but my fingerprints will be on the creamer bottle. Oh no, you did wash the cups didn't you?"

"No, I just rinsed them out like Betty would. Those cops won't know Betty didn't die in the dumpster."

"They ain't stupid, Marianne. I heard that sergeant sent cops up to her apartment to make sure nobody else went in there."

"They would do that no matter how she died. Don't you ever watch TV cop shows?"

"Yes, that's why I know how those guys think. Maybe I should skedaddle. I'll just tell Linda that I got a better offer somewhere else. Maybe in another state. I'm really good fixin' things, so I could find a job anywhere. You can stay here and let me know how it is goin'. We got our cell phones so we can keep in touch. Then when the cops don't find what

they are looking for, you can give your notice and come live with me."
Nick was talking so fast Marianne had a hard time understanding him.

She shook her head and said, "Nick, that is the dumbest thing I ever heard. Everyone would wonder why you left so fast."

"Marianne, this is all your fault. If you hadn't screwed up when we went to get her body, I wouldn't have to worry about any of this."

Marianne could have drilled a hole in Nick's head with the laser beams shooting out of her eyes. "Oh, sure, everything is my fault. I never told you to kill Betty. You didn't even tell me until after you did it. Maybe you should have planned better when you came up with this hair-brained idea. How was I supposed to know how you did it? When you told me you were going to take care of Betty and she would never make fun of me again, how was I to know you meant you were going to kill her?"

Detective Scott listened carefully when I relayed the conversation I had heard and then noted, "I am not surprised that this Marianne person was involved. Just goes to show you that you don't need a PhD. to commit a serious crime. In fact, often it is more likely someone thinks they are smarter than the police and could never be caught. We are not talking about white-collar crime in this situation. By the way, did you know before this that she and Nick were related?"

"No, nobody knew. I am not even sure that Linda knew. Because their last names are different it would never occur to anyone that they were siblings," I said.

"Well, now that we know how it happened and who was responsible, we just need proof to take to the DA. You mentioned before that you might have the proof we would need to bring the guilty party to justice. What did you mean by that?"

"When Nick and I had coffee, he put something in my coffee creamer while I was in the kitchen. That is the only time we were not together that night, and it was the only thing on the coffee table besides the coffee cups. I added the coffee carafe to the table and then went back for the pie. He would have had access to the coffee creamer for at least a couple of minutes while I was cutting the pie."

Detective Scott shared with me that she was not aware the weapon used in my demise was poison because she hadn't gotten a copy of the toxicology report yet. She stated the CSI teams had gone over my apartment with a fine-tooth comb and had removed everything in the refrigerator, the sink, and the bathroom. Detective Scott was beginning to believe they were going to be able to solve this case and undoubtedly, bring the criminals to trial, depending upon what evidence was found in my apartment of course.

The detectives returned to their car to discuss what they each had discovered. Detective Lindley said, "After talking to several people in the building and not getting anywhere, I think we need to find out what evidence was gathered in the apartment. I know it will take some time to receive any results, so the best thing we can do is to continue interviewing everyone."

It was two days later when the detectives returned to Eden Estates. Detective Lindley told Linda they needed to continue interviewing people.

After I told Detective Scott what I remembered about Marianne and Nick, she decided she wanted to interview Nick herself. I followed her down to the maintenance room where Nick was adding bags of water softener salt to an enormous tank. When she entered the room, Nick was startled and dropped one of the bags into the tank.

"Oh, damn, you scared me," he shouted. "You shouldn't sneak up on people like that. You could give someone a heart attack."

"Mr. Olson, may I have a few minutes of your time, please?" asked Detective Scott much too politely, I thought.

"What do you want me for? Is somethin' broken you want fixed?"

"Not at this time. I just need to ask you a few questions about what happened here on Monday. I would like us to go into the computer room so we could have some privacy? Are you free now?"

"Well, I have to crawl into this here tank to get the bag of salt that I dropped in there. Then we can go." Nick went to the back of the room and brought out a step ladder which he used to gain access to the top of the tank. Thankfully, the tank was almost full of salt so he had no trouble retrieving the bag. Detective Scott did however notice that when Nick bent over into the tank he had "plumber's crack" because his pants didn't cover his entire rear end. She looked away and pretended to be very interested in the furnace.

When they were both seated in the computer room, Nick seemed very nervous and kept reaching into his shirt pocket for a cigarette. Detective Scott reminded him he couldn't smoke in the building, and he said, "Oh, yeah, I sometimes forget."

Detective Scott tried to put him at ease by starting out asking him about his duties as a maintenance person.

"Well, I take care of all the apartments when something breaks or needs fixing. I change a lot of light bulbs and unstop a lot of toilets. I don't know what these old people try to flush down there, but they sure have a lot of trouble with them toilets. I also paint the apartments and clean the carpet when people move out. Sometimes, they don't even clean the fridge out or scrub the floors." He shook his head and said, "Some people just don't care what I hafta go through when they live like pigs."

It sounded to Detective Scott like Nick was rambling, which happens a lot when people are nervous about talking to the police. "OK, getting back to the problem at hand, can you tell me where you were on Sunday night?" Detective Scott asked. She noticed a definite change in Nick's demeanor. As soon as she asked him that question, he squirmed in his chair and the color drained from his face. He turned a definite shade of ash.

"Well, I guess I was at home watching TV. I can't remember what I watched because I sometimes fall asleep if the show is boring."

"What did you do on Sunday, anything special?"

"Um, after church I went out for breakfast with some friends at the Perkin's in Green Bay, the one on the north side of the lake. Then I went to Menards and picked up some paint brushes and plastic that I use when I paint. After that I watched some wrestlin' on TV. The Gouger was on, and I like watching him put people's eyes out. It's really funny. I know it ain't real because they all come back the next week, but it is funny anyway. I thought about being a wrestler, but I'm too skinny."

Detective Scott knew she was getting the run around but she was determined to get the answers to her questions. "Again, what were you doing on Sunday night, Mr. Olson?"

"Like I said, probably watching TV."

"Well, Mr. Olson, I have it on good authority that you were cleaning an empty apartment on Sunday night because someone was going to move in on Monday."

"Oh, yeah, I guess that was Sunday night. I forgot."

"Did you see any of the residents while you were working?"

"No, I put my radio on when I am working, so I don't see or hear nobody."

"Well, thank you very much, Mr. Olson. I would like to get your address and phone number in case we have further questions."

"Whatever," said Nick, and he rattled off the information while Detective Scott wrote it in her notebook.

Knowing what Detective Scott knew to be true about Mrs. Nelson's death, she had to tell Detective Lindley what she knew in order for this investigation to move forward. It didn't make any sense to continue to interview the other residents when she knew it was a waste of time.

Detective Scott started looking around the building for her partner and remembered he had said he would be on the first floor interviewing people. She found him coming out of an apartment at the end of the hallway. She waved to him indicating she wanted to talk to him before he knocked on another door.

"I think we should go out to the car and have a discussion about something I found out."

As Detective Lindley was walking along beside her in the parking lot, she said, "Well, have you fared any better than you did this morning?" I followed them out to their car.

"Not a lot." He said, "How about you?" The detectives proceeded to their car and rolled the windows down to let in some breeze while they waited for the AC to kick in.

"I don't think I will find out anything else here. The further I went down the hall, the more dementia I run into," said Detective Lindley. "One man thought that a UFO had landed on the roof and aliens had come in here and killed Mrs. Nelson. He said that beings from other planets could open locked doors and move around without making a sound so nobody would know they were there."

Detective Scott laughed because some of her interviews were just as ludicrous as his had been. She then said, "Remember when we first started this case and you asked me if I had special powers where I could see or speak to the dead?"

"Yes, I am really sorry I brought that up. Sometimes rumors float around a police station, and I should have known someone was just pulling my leg, being new in the department and all. And it was nice for you to go along with the joke." He looked somewhat embarrassed.

"It isn't just rumors, it's true. I do have special gifts where I can receive thoughts from people who have passed on. I can also see the auras of living people. That is how I can tell who is lying to me and who is telling the truth. If they display pink or white auras while I am questioning them, I know they are telling me the truth because they aren't good liars. But, if it is brown or black it means they are deceitful and are trying to hide something from me. There are a few people here that I could have cut their aura with a knife. It comes in handy when I am investigating a crime. Even if someone is not the perpetrator, it is still good to know who is lying and who's not."

"That is amazing but we still have to find proof that someone committed a crime, how they did it, and how we are going to prove it."

"I know. That is why I always hope the victim's spirit has decided to stay around after a crime has been committed. I can get an idea of who is lying, but we need to get some collaborating evidence from the victim. Many times, I can get them to talk to me and give me information. They don't always want to remain behind and are happy to just go on to wherever they go. But this time, Betty Nelson's spirit did stay behind, and she has told me exactly what transpired the night she died."

"What do you mean? She talked to you? Can you actually hear her voice?"

"No, it isn't like that. I can hear her thoughts, not her actual voice. It is so hard to explain to people what it is like. All I know is when a spirit is around me I am able to tune into their thoughts and feelings. I can ask them questions and get answers by listening to what they are thinking."

Detective Lindley looked skeptical. "Well, it isn't that I don't believe you, Scott, but you know we need to find the proof and be able to explain how we found it to the DA. We can't just say that we heard a voice or felt a spirit."

"I know, I know. Just listen to what I learned from Mrs. Nelson." Detective Scott retold everything she had heard from Betty Nelson.

When she was finished telling the tale, Detective Lindley shook his head and laughed. "Wow, do you really believe this story? And even if we do, how are we going to explain how we were able to discover the evidence?"

Detective Scott said, "Once we receive the lab reports and fingerprint evidence from the apartment, it will be clear we have to fingerprint everyone in the building. Then we can prove Nick put the poison in the creamer because only his and Mrs. Nelson's prints will be on the bottle and the coffee cups."

"But, Marianne's will be there too if what you heard was true," said Detective Lindley. "Didn't Mrs. Nelson tell you that Marianne put the creamer in the fridge and the cups in the sink when she and Nick came to retrieve the body?"

"You're right. So how are we going to prove it was Nick and not Marianne who supplied the poison?"

"Well, we have to search for the poison container and see if both of their prints are on it, or just Nick's."

Chapter 34
The Bus Trip

Even though time had no meaning for me, I was getting antsy to know what was going on with the investigation, so I decided to travel to the police station for an update. There were several methods I could us to reach my destination and gave it some serious thought. After examining all of the options, I decide doing it the old fashioned way would be best. I would take the bus.

Luckily for me, there was a bus stop right outside the front door of Eden Estates, so I gathered with the other people waiting patiently. It was fun to observe them without them knowing. I felt like a voyeur. One man was looking at his phone, and, I am sure unconsciously, scratching his crotch, picking his nose, and passing gas with abandon. The others were just as self consumed. I wondered what happened to the days when we would make conversation with people while we were waiting ~~with~~ in line. Ain't technology great?

When the bus finally came, I let all of the other riders board the bus first. By the time I entered, there were no seats available so I looked around for the least approachable person I could see. He was a long, lean man who looked to be in his early twenties with a green mohawk (purple was so yesterday it seemed) and more jewelry on his face than I had in my jewelry box. I sat down on his lap. He looked up from his phone and shivered noticeably. Looking around, when he saw no one near him, he settled down and returned to his phone.

I was scanning the bus for other interesting people when I heard a child ask her mother, "Why is that lady sitting on that man's lap?"

Her mother looked up at the other passengers and asked, "Who are you talking about, Rachel?"

"That lady over there sitting on that guy's lap."

"You must be imagining things. There is no one sitting on anyone's lap."

"Yes, there is, and she is smiling at me." Susie waved at me, and I returned the favor.

So, it seems some people are actually able to see ghosts. I hadn't considered that possibility. Maybe it was just children because they have not been tainted by the real world yet. Interesting. It may be fun to go to a place where a lot of children are present to test my theory. It could be entertaining to have children talking to me and me to them, and having their parents wonder what in the world was happening to little Joshua and Tiffany. Food for thought.

The bus arrived at my stop, and the door to the police station was just steps away, so I went through the door (and I mean *through* the door). The building was old, like maybe 80 or 90 years old, so it had all of the art deco molding and a long wooden staircase leading to the upper floors. The main floor was marble and had grooves where millions of feet had trod these halls for nearly a century. I loved it.

Since I couldn't very well ask for directions, I looked around at various doors finally finding one with a window in the top half and gold lettering saying, "Marin County Homicide Division". This is where I wanted to be. As I entered the room, I took in the scene before me. There were many people of all shapes and color, in the standard blue police uniform with the only exception being the marking on their shirts to tell what rank they were. Multiple green metal desks holding computers and other office equipment filled most of the space. It looked like a sea of blue. I was wondering to myself, with this many police around how come I could have been murdered in my own apartment. I had never been in a police station before so this was very interesting to me. It appeared the higher ranking officers had offices around the outside perimeter of the room because most of them wore uniforms with higher ranks and several wore suits.

I heard a woman speaking to one of the police officers in the large room as she sat next to his desk in an older wooden chair. "I wasn't anywhere near my ex-husband's office yesterday. I am not supposed to bother him so I don't."

The office said, "Then how do you explain your car, and your face showing up on the closed circuit camera about 5 o'clock?"

"Well, I may have been just passing by. I can't remember my own name some days so how am I supposed to remember what I did yesterday?"

"Ma'ma, this is the second warning we have given you in as many weeks. If continue to ignore the restraining order, there will be severe consequences, do you understand?"

Reluctantly, she said, "Yes."

I decided some of the people in the offices were probably detectives because they wore suits instead of the standard uniform, so I moved in that direction. In one office on the left side of the room, I found my quarry. I spotted Detectives Lindley and Scott examining a computer screen on one of the desks. I could tell Detective Scott was aware of my presence and tried to hide that fact because she didn't want Detective Lindley to notice her shift in posture. I perched on top of a file cabinet so I could peek over their shoulders to see what they were gazing at. I started bouncing my foot up and down as I became more comfortable with my position. I almost lost my shoe when it slipped to the end of my toes, but I caught myself.

Detective Lindley nodded his head and commented, "Well, well, well. This is very interesting. Three sets of prints were discovered on the creamer bottle and the coffee cups. One set is Mrs. Nelson's, of course, and one was unidentified. But I am most interested in the other print. Look who it belongs to. Nick Olson, the maintenance man at Eden Estates. I wonder why his criminal history didn't show up in his background check when he was hired."

Detective Scott guessed, "Maybe he wasn't given a background check. Sometimes management ignores the law and hires someone they know. We will have to look into that little matter. In any case we need to set up a time for the fingerprint technicians to go to Eden Estates and gather the evidence we need. I will call the lab and find out when they will be available."

"OK, then I will call Mrs. Carmichael and tell her when the techs will be there, but I won't disclose the reason why. I don't want to give her a heads up yet," said Detective Lindley.

When Detective Scott called the lab, he was happy they could send a team to the apartment building the next day. She then called Linda Carmichael and informed her some technicians would be visiting her the next day to gather some more evidence. Linda asked why. "Haven't you collected everything you need in the past several times you have been here? What kind of evidence do you still need?"

"The technicians will explain everything when they arrive," Detective Scott informed her.

"Well, tomorrow is my day off, but if you insist, I can meet you there at 8:00am." Linda did not sound happy.

The technicians arrived promptly at 8:00am. Linda escorted them to her office. They introduced themselves and told her they were there to collect fingerprints from some of the people in the building including herself and her staff. Since Linda's office was cramped, at best, they asked if there was another room they could use to collect what they needed, away from the office, lobby and mailboxes. They said they wanted to disrupt as few people as possible.

Linda took them to the computer room so they could set up their equipment. She was informed they would start with her and her staff before calling in any of the residents.

"Are you really going to take fingerprints from these vulnerable people? They already don't feel safe here. They will feel like criminals."

One of the technicians explained, "I am sorry ma'am but this is a necessary procedure in order to eliminate suspects. This shouldn't take a very long time, and we will be gone by the end of day."

"Fine."

Linda sat down at one of the tables, and the procedure started. The technicians explained how this process would work. "We will press four fingers of the right hand on the surface of the electronic card, making sure that the fingers are held together during the process. Then we will do the same with the left hand, and then do both thumbs. The process only takes a few minutes and has the highest degree of accuracy. Plus, the residents would not have to get their hands full of ink on their hands that would occur if we used the paper and ink method."

After Linda was done, the techs asked to see Nick Olson. Linda called him and asked him to come to the computer room. He seemed extremely nervous and was not as cooperative as Linda had been. The technicians had to try several times to capture the images and finally were able to gather the required information.

Linda called Jeff Peters, the caretaker, and explained to him what was going to transpire. He seemed a little nervous, but nothing compared to what Nick had been. The technicians then told Linda they would need to see the following residents: Marianne, Carol, Tootsie, Alice, JoAnn, Noreen, Jennifer, Genevieve and Lorraine.

As they took turns coming to the computer room, their faces looked starkly different when they entered than when they left. Marianne and her tribe were mad as hornets spewing curse words all the way down the hall. My friends looked relieved something was finally getting done on this case.

When the technicians left Eden Estates with the evidence they required, the building was abuzz with activity. Many of the residents gathered in the community room to compare notes about what had transpired that day. Several of the people who were not included in the investigation felt snubbed, instead of lucky.

Nancy complained, "I have always been as nice to Betty as Tootsie or JoAnn. How come they are getting all of the attention?"

Alice agreed with Nancy. "They are also questioning all of the people who hated her. I can understand that but don't they think her friends have anything important to say? They hardly asked me any questions when they came to my apartment. I asked them several, but they kept their traps shut. Did any of you tell the cops about how mean Marianne was to Betty? I did." Alice laughed and said, "I told them about what happens in the community room between the nice people and the mean people, and they seemed very interested. By the way, what did you think of the detectives?"

Just then, Angela dragged a chair up to the table and since she had overheard the question, and thought she was included in the query, she shared her opinion. "I thought Detective Lindley was delicious. I could have licked him down to his bones, but couldn't tell if he was really interested. I guess he must have thought the difference in our ages was just too much to deal with, but I did think he was attracted to me because he held my hand just a little too long when he shook it. You know what I mean. He was sort of standoffish at first. What do cops always say, 'Just the facts, ma'am, just the facts.' I thought Detective Scott was kind of flighty. She kept looking around my apartment as if she expected to find another person there, but of course it was only the three of us."

After listening to Angela, several others made comments about the detectives, and the conversation went astray. Most of them were off and running, gossiping about everyone else in the building.

Chapter 35

The Fun Begins

A couple of days later the fingerprint evidence results were in, and Detectives Lindley and Scott were reviewing the reports. I was watching from on top of a potted plant that hadn't seen water since the Clinton administration.

Detective Lindley was smiling and shaking his head. He said, "Why am I not surprised? The evidence proves what we already suspected. Both Nick and Marianne's fingerprints were found on the creamer bottle and the coffee cups in Mrs. Nelson's apartment. Marianne's were also found on several other items in her apartment like the refrigerator door and kitchen faucet."

Detective Scott offered her opinion on the new evidence. "I think the next step will to be to gather DNA evidence from Nick to prove beyond a shadow of a doubt that he drank from the coffee cup we found in the apartment."

Detective Lindley agreed, "Let's go surprise Nick and ask for a cheek swab. If he won't give one voluntarily, we will need to get another warrant."

"I don't think we should give him a heads-up. If he won't volunteer his DNA, then he will know we will be back with a warrant and maybe he will flee. With the fingerprint evidence, we should be able to get a warrant, so I suggest we get that before we surprise him at work."

"You're right. Let's give Judge Sullivan a call and run it by her. We may be able to get one today if we play our cards right."

I wanted to be in the building when the detectives dropped the bombshell on Nick, so I hitched a ride on a bicycle that was going my way. When we arrived near the apartment building, I flew the rest of the way and right through the door. I sat right outside Linda's office so I wouldn't miss a thing.

When The detectives were able to secure a warrant for Nick Olson's DNA, they headed over to Eden Estates along with a lab technician to actually take the sample. They also had another warrant to search Nick's home and property. When they rang the office, Linda opened the door and asked what she could do to help them, again. Detective Scott explained they needed to see Mr. Olson. Linda called him and requested he come to the office at once.

When Nick appeared in the office doorway and saw the detectives, they could see him stiffen up and a nasty scowl registered on his face. They asked him if they could go to the maintenance room and talk for a few minutes.

"What the hell is this about?" Nick nearly shouted. "I gave you my fingerprints already. I don't think I'll do nothin' else to help you. You are just trying to find someone to blame for this murder and because I got a record you want to pick on me."

Linda's head snapped up from her paperwork and glared at Nick. "What do you mean you have a record? I assume you mean a criminal record, is that right? How come that didn't show up on your background report? I knew nothing about this."

"Well, I didn't really have a background check when Sylvia hired me because she knew my sister, Marianne, and Marianne said I was OK and I could fix anything."

"Nick, you will cooperate in any way necessary with law enforcement, is that clear?"

"I guess so," mumbled Nick.

All three peace officers followed Nick and moved across the hall to the maintenance room, and Detective Lindley closed the door. When the search warrant was pulled the out of his pocket and presented to Nick, he started to shake. He was told the warrant was for a sample of his DNA. Nick sat down heavily on a rickety stool near a makeshift desk.

"There ain't no way you are taking any of my blood," shouted Nick

"We will not be taking any of your blood, sir," the technician said. "Just open your mouth wide, and we will swab the inside of your cheek. It will take about ten seconds. Do you understand what I am going to do?"

Nick moved farther away from the technician and clamped his mouth shut until his cheeks turned red. He said through clenched teeth, "You're not sticking that thing down my throat. I gag easy. Do you want me to toss my biscuits right on your nice jacket?"

The technician repeated the instructions to Nick, but he refused to open his mouth.

Detective Scott injected herself into the conversation by saying, "If we can't get this done here and now, we will need to call a squad car which will take you down to the station where, I guarantee, there are very large officers who will make sure you open your mouth. It could prove to be embarrassing to you for all of the residents to see you being put into a police car, but it is up to you. We can do this the easy way or the hard way. Now, which way is it going to be?"

Nick, reluctantly, opened his mouth and observed the lanyard hanging from the technician's neck. To him, it looked very official and scary. The inside of Nick's mouth looked like the Sahara Desert. "Do you have any water in this room, Mr. Olson?" Detective Lindley asked.

"Yeah, I got some in that little fridge in the back," stammered Nick.

Detective Scott moved right in front of Nick and said very plainly (about three inches from his face), "Go get the water and drink as much as you can while I count to thirty."

Surprisingly, Nick did exactly what he was told. When Detective Scott had counted to thirty, she said, "Now, open wide." It looked like Nick was really afraid of Detective Scott because he obeyed her again. The technician was able to get the sample he needed, went out into the hall, and took a patrol car that had been waiting for him back to the lab.

It seemed in situations like this that Nick was more afraid of Detective Scott than he was her partner. I wondered why that was. Maybe because he was used to being bossed around by women in his life and knew what could happen if he tried to stick up for himself.

I thought, "Boy, this guy has been bossed around by women and bullied all of his life. No wonder he is such a mess."

Detective Scott picked up on my thoughts and looked a little sad too. She knew criminals were not born, but created by the circumstances in which they were forced to live.

"Thank you for your cooperation, Mr. Olson," Detective Scott said politely.

Detective Lindley addressed his partner and requested they speak privately. They left the building and sat on the patio where they could be alone. "I think we now have to concentrate on how we can find the container that held the poison. We need to prove Nick's prints are also on the container if we are going to take this matter to the District Attorney (DA)."

"Now we need to use the warrant we have to continue searching Eden Estates, so let's get some CSIs back over here to search the out buildings and anywhere else we feel we need to look through."

Detective Scott had requested and received a warrant to search Nick's home, storage area and any other property used by Nick. The detectives returned to the building and looked for Nick so that they could serve him with the warrant to search is home and property.

When the detectives, along with three CSIs, entered the building again, it wasn't hard to find Nick. They found him still in the work room on the first floor. Detective Lindley surprised him while he was repairing a window screen. "Mr. Olson, we have a warrant to search your home."

Nick jumped when he saw who was in the room with. "What do you mean, you're gonna search my home? You ain't got no right to hassle me like this. I can't leave right now because I have lots of these screens to fix. The people are complaining 'cause the skeeters are getting in."

Detective Scott told Nick that either he could accompany them to his house, or just give them the keys and they would conduct the search without him being present.

"Well," Nick said. "If you put it that way, I guess I want to be there with you. Linda went home so she won't even know if I leave for a while."

Two CSIs were left at Eden Estates with the understanding there was no public space that was not going to be searched.

The detectives followed Nick to his house and parked on the street. I had taken this opportunity to again ride to the next destination instead of flying. I stood on the top of the car with my arms extended above my head and felt like I was in a grade-B movie where all inhibitions had been ignored. It was wonderful. The CSIs came in their own vehicle with a mobile laboratory.

Unfortunately, for Nick, there was large lettering on the side of their van stating, "MAREN POLICE LAB".

Trish and Andy, two of the CSIs, split up to cover more ground. One went into the house, and one opened the garage door. Another one asked Nick for the key to the outbuildings.

Nick lived on a suburban, on- acre piece of property that hadn't seen a lawn mower in recent months. The rest of the neighborhood was properly maintained with manicured lawns, recently clipped hedges, and flower beds that would make a master gardener proud. I was kind of surprised at the condition of the house and yard considering Nick kept Eden Estates running smoothly and repaired at all times. Maybe he decided he had enough of fixing things at his place of employment and just wanted to relax when he got home.

The house was the typical ranch style three bedroom, one and a half bath house with a family room on the lower level. I had never seen a TV that large and never understood why single men thought they needed a television the size of a wall with three or four gaming systems connected. Two male CSIs were oohing and ahhing over the set up with the speakers lining the ceiling that could probably blast a hole in an eardrum. I guess it was true after all — size does matter. Detective Lindley had to reminded them they were here to search the residence, not covet the owner's toys. They continued their search.

Upstairs the kitchen and dining room were being searched, and Nick was pacing back and forth nibbling on his fingernails. When Nancy Perkins, one of the CSIs, came out of one bedroom with a zip lock bag containing what looked to be a nice supply of pot, Nick fell onto the couch and groaned.

Detective Lindley said they should just put it on the folding card table that served as they only eating area on the first level of the house. Even though marijuana use in Wisconsin was illegal, the CSIs were looking for a different incriminating substance. Most of the furniture looked like it had been scavenged from the dump. There were no pictures on the wall, no end tables, or other places to sit. Two mismatched lamps were elevated off the floor by miss-matched plastic crates college students normally used for bookcases. The only appliances in the kitchen that looked to have had any use were the refrigerator and the microwave. The stove was piled with old mail, some of which was falling on the floor. It was apparent that no gourmet cooking went on in this house. The trash can was overflowing with pizza boxes and beer bottles. Even though Nick was at least fifty years old, he still lived like a teenager.

The detectives left the house and crossed the back yard to an outbuilding. Just as one CSI was giving a report to Detective Lindley about what had been found or not found, Detective Scott received a call on her cell phone. She ended her call and told Detective Lindley they were being called back to Eden Estates. Something had happened that needed their attention.

Not waiting for the slowness of a squad car, I closed my eyes and thought I was back at Eden Estates. All of a sudden, I was standing in the community room where several people were playing bingo. When the detectives arrived, a CSI met them at their car and led them back to a storage shed next to the air conditioning unit. There was much commotion in the shed.

Tom Wilson, who was leading the search for the container of rat poison came over to the detectives and told them a story that was so strange it had to be true. "Lindley, you won't believe what happened here a few minutes ago. I was going through the shed looking in all of the boxes, bags, and tin cans I could find. The last place I needed to check was on top of the boards in the rafters that formed a sort of ceiling. I took a rake and was moving the boards so that I could climb up on a step stool and poke my head up there. All of a sudden this granular, blue substance started showering down on my head. If I didn't wear glasses I probably would have gotten some in my eyes. I reached up into the space and found a plastic bag with an oblong tin can inside. After I retrieved it, I noticed the plastic bag had probably been eaten through by a mouse or raccoon. That is why the contents were spilling out of the bag. I was hopeful this was what we were searching for. But I didn't get really excited until I saw skull and crossbones on the can and a label said, "Poison, not for human consumption." The label also says it is for killing rodents and should be handled with gloves."

Detective Lindley smiled broadly. He said, "I can only hope the person who used this product did not follow those instructions and a clear set of fingerprints will be apparent when we take it back to the lab. Great job, Tom. You always make this look so easy."

"Thanks a lot. It isn't really that this job is easy, but stupid criminals sure make me look good."

Tom collected the other members of his team and they were laughing all the way to their vehicle when they heard the story about how this evidence was found.

The detectives returned to their car and followed the mobile laboratory back to the police station. They called the CSIs at Nick's house and asked if they had found anything remotely like rat poison. They were told no so Detective Lindley instructed them to stop the search for today. If necessary they could return another day. Detective Scott wanted to be happy about the find Tom had made but she knew she had to wait until the rat poison can was finished being processed.

Chapter 36
The Evidence

In the next few days, a lot was happening around Eden Estates. Linda instructed workman to replace the carpeting, apply new paint to all of the walls, and even change the shades on the windows. I heard Linda talking to some of the residents about all of these major changes. She explained, "All of the things being replaced in apartment 304 have been needed for a long time. I am just taking this opportunity with it being vacant to accomplish the needed repairs."

At the coffee time in the community room the changes were a major topic of conversations. Tootsie asked her friends at the table, "I wonder if Linda is going to tell people looking at Betty's apartment that she not only died there, but was murdered. I think they need to tell people before they sign the lease. I would like to know if it was me."

JoAnn added, "I bet they don't have to tell new people because others have died in their apartments, and I bet they didn't tell anyone then."

The most conspicuous change in the community room was Marianne's behavior. She sat at a table farthest away from the others and talked quietly with her friends. No historyonics, no outbursts, no advice giving. Everyone noticed these changes and wondered what was going on with her.

Alice offered her ideas about this situation, "Maybe she really does have a soul and feels bad about how terrible she treated Betty. No, I guess not. That would mean she also has a conscience, which of course, she doesn't." Alice went on, "I heard the best rumor in the hallway yesterday. I accidently overheard Linda talking to someone in her office while I was getting my mail. Her door was wide open, so I couldn't help hearing her." Alice at least had the decency to blush. "Linda was saying something about Marianne and Nick being related. Do you think that could be true?"

Tootsie nodded her head when Alice was speaking and said, "He does seem to spend more time in her apartment than anywhere else. Maybe that is why everything in her apartment gets fixed before anyone else's does. I bet this rumor is true."

I left this gossip session to check on what was going on at the Maren Police Department. I climbed into a taxi heading in the right direction. When I arrived, I went into the room where the detectives worked. There was a feeling of electricity in the room, and I assumed it was concerning my case. Listening to Detective Scott it sounded like something big was happening.

"Look at this data, Lindley. It says Nick Olson's fingerprints and DNA were the only ones present on the can of rat poison." She smiled at detective Lindley and said, "We've got him. And since Marianne's fingerprints were also on the creamer and cups in the sink, we also have her."

Detective Lindley said, "OK, it's time we took this to the DA and obtained warrants for their arrests. I feel like Mrs. Nelson is finally going to get justice."

"And, she will have the last word on Marianne. I know she is going to feel good about that."

Detective Scott did not tell her partner that she could hear me laughing and yahooing all over the office. I told her I was going to be at their trial and enjoy every minute of it.

Detective Lindley noticed the big smile on Detective Scott's face and said, "Now, don't tell me Mrs. Nelson is here with us right now."

"OK, I won't, but she is actually."

"Well, tell her she can follow us down to the DA's office if she wants to. She may enjoy watching the start of the process that will get her revenge for what those two degenerates put her through."

Scott chuckled, "I don't have to tell her, because you just did."

The detectives collected all of the documents that would provide Carl Thomas, the District Attorney, with enough evidence for him to indict Nick Olson and Marianne Taylor for my murder. I couldn't believe that something was actually going to happen to bring some peace to me and the other residents as well. I was wondering what Marianne's friends would say about this situation.

Chapter 37
The Final Chapter

The next thing I knew, Nick and Marianne were being handcuffed and seated in two separate squad cars as the residents and other staff at Eden Estates lined the inside of the community room windows and the outdoor patio. At first everyone was surprised and then glee set in. Several people actually applauded when the accused were taken away, giving each other high-fives and laughing until they were bent over and could hardly catch their breath. It was wonderful to be here to witness this.

I was wondering what was next for me. What would I do now? I hoped I wouldn't be spending eternity at Eden Estates.

Just then I looked across the parking lot between the stone pillars that indicated where the driveway was located. I saw someone walking towards me. They seemed familiar somehow. As they moved closer I began thinking for some reason, this person was here for me. By the time he was ten feet away I could tell it was Larry, my late husband who had died three years ago. He looked ten years younger than he had when he died — healthy and happy. He held out his hand and said, "Hi honey, I've come to take you home with me." I ran into his arms and received the warmest of hugs. I missed this so much since his passing and started to believe I may never see him again. We turned around towards the street and walked across the lawn hand in hand. The farther we moved away from Eden Estates, the more people I saw coming toward me. Many had been gone for decades — my parents and old friends. It was so nice to be reunited in what I was hoping was heaven.